Paws
for
Christmas

MARIAH LYNNE

ISBN: 978-1-953735-03-4

Published by Satin Romance
An Imprint of Melange Books, LLC
White Bear Lake, MN 55110
www.satinromance.com

Published in the United States of America.

Cover Design by Caroline Andrus

To Sam my real life big scruffy brown dog surrendered to a shelter at nine months old, but he like the Sam in the book had a happy life. We adopted him and he remained our buddy for fifteen years.

And to my husband Jerry for his love and encouragement.

CHAPTER 1

Mrs. Amanda Sonaro, wearing a purple and yellow flowered Muumuu, stood under the green and red silk Christmas garlands that dangled from the Island Pharmacy's navy blue awning, chatting with her two friends. All three women, noted island gossips, waited for someone to pass or something to happen that they could talk about. Knowing from experience what they were up to, I brushed by them as fast as I could to go inside and buy shampoo. As I did, I noticed Mrs. Sonaro push her pink round sunglasses to the tip of her nose to study me.

"Well look at that!" I overheard her tell her friends. "Jessica Monroe's wearing bright red lipstick! Not her usual pale pink. Bet she didn't change her shade for Christmas so maybe that's a sign she's finally getting over her ex, Jake, and has a new man in her life."

When you live on a small Florida Gulf Coast barrier island like I do, a change in lipstick shades can send some island residents into a gossip feeding frenzy. Not wanting to confront her, I answered mentally. Yes, my lipstick shade is now red, and it is for Christmas. There is no new man in my life.

I returned home from the pharmacy wondering how much of their nonsense I'll have to deny, but I didn't let that disrupt my holiday plans. Today, November 23rd, is the day after Thanksgiving and the day I traditionally start my holiday decorating. I've lived on Hibiscus Island my entire life and appreciate my life here, but this year more than ever, I wanted to put this Christmas season on pause even though I knew I needed some Christmas cheer in my own life now more than ever.

Needless to say, last month was not Currier and Ives perfect for me. My fiancé, Jake, an emergency room physician, left me for a nurse, while a few weeks later I had to put my beautiful but very sick angel Mazy, a cocker spaniel, to sleep. I miss her more than ever. I can't say that about that double-timing Jake.

Since our island's main tourist season doesn't start until Christmas Day, we weren't flooded with visitors. My work as an associate editor and contributing writer for a national online travel magazine, *Dream Travel*, usually comes to a standstill this time of year so I decided to use my extra free time to decorate my home and get ready for my annual Christmas Eve open house in style hoping to bring some cheer to myself and other islanders who needed it as well.

May be overkill, but I decorated my white front door with a handmade huge shiny silver tinsel wreath with attached cut-out cardboard hot pink flamingos and wrapped in white snowflake lights. After I hung the wreath, I attached chasing white lights along the beams of my porch before planting pink poinsettias in the pots that line my front walk. To insure I had enough cheer, I outlined my front door frame with silver garlands that matched the wreath.

Taking a few steps back from my pink island cottage to admire my work, I came to a sudden halt when I heard loud continuous barking. I turned surprised to find the dirtiest big brown dog I have ever seen. He barked and stared straight at me. I didn't recognize this dog as a local pet since I had never seen him before.

Our island is a small town before all the tourists invade so most of us islanders can identify local pets and kids. Not knowing if he was friendly or aggressive, I tried to shoo him away at first, but he wouldn't leave. This big brown dog remained steadfast as my eyes examined him further; he was thin almost emaciated. What I could see of his golden-brown fur was matted and filthy. I love animals especially dogs and wanted to assist him. As I looked into his gentle light brown eyes, my heart melted. This poor guy cried out for my help so I decided to talk to him.

"Okay, easy boy. I'm not going to hurt you." When he heard the soft tone of my voice, he stopped barking for a few minutes and wagged his tail. Normally tail wagging would be a good sign, but I remembered my friend Tom had a watchdog, Specter, in his auto repair garage. Specter would wag his tail before he was ready to bite so all that sweet looking tail wagging didn't convince me. I spoke to the dog again like I was talking to a child. "Honestly, honey, in all of my thirty-one years, I've never seen a dirtier dog than you. I'm not going to hurt you. You look like a good boy."

At that point, he dropped down on my lawn and placed his head in his paws. He appeared weak and whined. Whined? Was he hurt? He was breathing hard. What do I do now? I felt so sorry for him, I had to approach him to try and help. I walked slowly toward him holding my hand out for him to sniff. He looked up at me with a most gentle gaze. I cautiously moved in closer to him and he licked my hand after smelling.

I petted his head and noticed he had on a leather harness and collar, but he had ripped through the leather leaving the skeleton of both wrapped around his body. I couldn't pick him up so I left him on the front lawn and ran inside to get a bowl of water and a bowl of plain Cheerios. I thought of

Cheerios because my Mazy used to love them and since she's been gone a few weeks now, I don't have any dog food in the house, having donated what was left to our local shelter.

I guessed by the dog's features he was part Golden Lab and part German Shepherd. This huge creature gulped down the bowl of water before turning to the Cheerios and eating the entire bowl. I dashed inside to get him more. It didn't take this guy very long to clean the second bowl as well. I didn't want to let him leave, especially if he was injured. He seemed like he had a bad go of something, but I didn't want to call the shelter. Poor guy looked like he'd been through enough and besides it was almost Christmas and I didn't want him spending the holiday in a cage so I decided to call Mazy's vet, Dr. Amy. I dialed the number still on my cell's call list.

"Dr. Amy's office. Susan speaking. How may I assist you?"

I responded, frantic for help. "Susan, this is Jessica Monroe. I need an appointment with Dr. Amy today if possible."

"Hey Jessica, nice to hear from you again. Are you getting a new pup for Christmas? We miss seeing you."

"No," I answered almost cutting Susan off. "I have a stray dog that wandered into my yard and needs medical attention. He's in pretty bad shape."

Susan placed me on hold for a few minutes before she came back on the line. "I checked with Dr. Amy. She said to bring him here in twenty minutes. We close at four. The office is slow right now because of the holidays. Most islanders don't want vet bills this time of year unless it's for an emergency."

"Please thank the doctor for me. We'll be there unless I can't lift him into my car."

Susan added. "See you then."

I hung up and felt something furry nudging my leg. It was my new friend. I looked at my watch. Three thirty? I had been so busy decorating I had no idea it was so late. I spotted an extra piece of rope I used to tie some downed palm fronds earlier in the day for trash pick-up. I grabbed the rope and made a noose out of it; one that I hoped would hold him to get to the vet. I placed it around the dog's neck and had him stand. He could and walked with me to my front door so I could lock it before we made our way over to my car, a red and white four door Mini Cooper, not exactly the right size for transporting a dog of his size.

Now for my next problem, will he be able get in on his own or will I have to give this big boy a lift? I opened the back door and tried coaxing him into my small back seat. Oh he was so dirty, and I just had my car detailed yesterday for the holiday parade. He looked at me. I had no doggie treats so all I could do was sweet talk him with "Good boy get in. Wanna go for a ride?"

Ride was the magic word. Wow he was one smart dog. He got in with no hesitation. I got in the driver's seat and just like that we were off to the island vet. As we drove through the island center, I wondered if Mrs. Sonaro and her chatty friends were still in front of the pharmacy and if they would notice my ruby red lipstick now or if that huge furry body in my back seat would dominate their gossip.

CHAPTER 2

My new furry companion and I arrived at Dr. Amy's right on time for our appointment. Her parking lot was empty, but I could see the lights were still on inside. Susan rushed out of the small peach colored stucco building to greet us. Her blue eyes opened as wide as moon pies when she saw who I had in my back seat. I opened the car door as Susan tried as hard as she could to stand back far enough from the dog's shaking off more of the caked mud and dirt from his fur to keep her uniform clean. That didn't work. Her immaculate cherry red striped uniform now had splatters of brown all across the front.

Looking a bit disgusted with all the dirt, Susan waved us in, still staying as far away from us as possible. She smirked, "Your poor car. Didn't I see you at the car wash yesterday? Anyway, please follow me inside. He's sure a lot bigger than Mazy. Where are you going to keep him in that tiny Beach cottage of yours?"

After listening to her snide remarks, I quipped. "I'm not keeping him. He's lost and I just want him to get checked."

Susan laughed, "Sure. Anything you say. When it comes to animals, we all know what a bleeding heart you are. When you go inside, please stand in the center of the waiting room. It will make it easier for me to clean the office after you leave. He is pretty dirty like he's been mud wrestling. I'll let Dr. Amy know you're here."

We did as we were asked. It only took a couple of minutes for my vet to come out and greet us. She took one look at the two of us and laughed. "Jessica, you're such a germaphobe and this dog looks like one big germ. Come on. Let's go into the exam room."

I felt like I've known Doc Amy forever. She has taken care of all of my pets since I was six. Now older with a touch of gray in her dark blonde hair, she walked a little slower than when I had first met her.

We followed, but she stopped suddenly like she had changed her mind. "On further thought, maybe we should get him bathed and groomed so I can take a real thorough look at him. I thought you weren't getting any more dogs after Mazy. You said you couldn't deal with the heartache of losing another pet."

I shook my head. "My Mazy was special. I can't replace her, and I can't stand the thought of losing another pet. He's here because he looks like he's been through a rough time. He wandered into my front yard lost, hungry, and needing care. I'll take care of him until I can locate his owner."

Dr. Amy smiled. "Of course, Jess. Of course you'll locate his owner. Whatever you say."

We went into the grooming area. Lucky Jeff was still there. He had on his African animal print smock and looked clean considering his job. The young handsome vet assistant took one look at my new friend and sighed. "I always liked a challenge."

Doc and I waited in the grooming waiting area that had a large glass window through which we could watch Jeff scrubbing the big guy with a long-bristled brush. The dog liked it. We realized this process could take a while but were patient to start the exam after this doggy spa treatment was finished. Jeff, holding his bather on a flimsy rope leash, followed us into an exam room. He told us. "This is the best I could do with what I had to work with. He was a challenge. Nice guy but I had to apply two rounds of flea shampoo and two rinses, one with a conditioner."

I couldn't help blurting out, "Wow. He looks great. He's at least two shades lighter, a handsome golden brown now." Jeff interrupted my compliment. "I washed his torn harness and collar as well and found this. It's a green bone shaped charm with his name, Sam, on it and a phone number to call in case he gets lost or hurt."

"You're amazing," I exclaimed. "May I see it?"

Dr. Amy put a quick kibosh on that idea. "Please give me that. I'd like to examine him while he's in a good mood. We'll look at that after I give you my medical opinion."

She had Sam walk back into the lobby and step on the scale. "A whopping eighty-nine pounds," she exclaimed. "Jeff, please take Sam back into exam room A and help me lift him onto the exam table."

They lifted Sam and had him lay down on the table. He wagged his tail like crazy so he must have liked all the human attention. The vet felt his neck glands, his stomach, looked in his ears and eyes. "I don't see anything wrong at first glance but I'm going to do blood work to check for heartworms or any other underlying conditions."

My face must have revealed my inner concerns. Dr. Amy calmed my fears. "Don't worry, Jess, I'm not going to charge you for this visit. This is charity work. I do some every month. I'm lucky to live here and lucky because I love what I do so I always try to help other pet owners who are not as fortunate or a stray animal in distress like Sam here."

I knew I loved her for a reason. Jeff hugged Sam's head while the vet drew a couple of vials of blood from above the inside of his paw. When she finished, Jeff held up his paw and

Dr. Amy bandaged it with white tape. Jeff then gave him some treats which he enjoyed beyond measure.

"Now, Jeff, help me get Sam back on the floor," Dr. Amy asked. "And I'll take a look at that collar."

They put him down gently and he walked over and sat down next to me as if he sensed I was trying to help him. Dr. Amy looked at the green bone shaped charm. "I tested him for a microchip but found none. Not every county requires them. I wish they did. It would make my job easier and provide the best way to connect a lost pet with its owner. Evidently, like Jeff told us, his name according to the plastic bone is Sam."

The vet called his name, "Hi, Sam. I see the phone number on your charm is a Florida phone number and even better, it's right here in Lee County."

She turned to me. "Jess, would you like me to notify the county animal services and have him housed at the shelter?"

I crossed my arms in defiance. "Thank you, but no. This guy will not end up in a cage, especially at Christmas time. I will call his owner's number myself."

The kind vet shook her head as she handed me his bone charm and ripped collar. "Okay, but who knows what can of worms you're about to open. There were no signs of abuse. He has some bruising but from a fall or an accident. Nothing unusual or extreme. You know at Christmas, some poor folks let their animals go because they can't afford to feed them. I have some bags of food under the Christmas tree in the waiting area. Please take two bags before you leave, and Jeff, please help get out a bag of biscuits for her."

Jeff nodded and met us in the front hall, adding, "You're going to need something stronger than one of our make-shift leashes. I have some extra heavy ones at home for my two big guys. I'll stop by your house after work and drop one off."

Jeff helped load the bags of food and treats in my front seat so I could get Sam in the back. "Thanks, Jeff. I appreciate this very much. In the meantime, I'm going to go home and try that number."

Jeff looked concerned. "Be careful. Remember what Dr. Amy said. You could be opening a can of worms."

With his warning in mind we left, driving home at dusk, through our small island business district all lit up with the town's Christmas lights. As soon as we pulled into my small driveway, Terry, my next-door neighbor, came running over, curious at who was in my backseat. "Okay, fill me in. Who's this handsome dude?"

I opened my window. "His name is Sam and I'm taking care of him for his owner. He's not mine so make sure you tell any and all curious onlookers that."

Terry cupped his eyes to peek in the back window. "Friendly?"

"Pretty much. Want to meet him? If so, stand back please so I can give Sam enough room to get out."

Terry followed my directions to the letter so I opened the back door. Sam bounced out wagging his tail and heading straight for Terry who gushed. "He's beautiful. He looks like he has just been groomed. From the parts I can see, I'd guess he's part German Shepherd. He has the same kind of ears except they're droopy and from the color of his fur and his light brown eyes Golden Lab."

"That was my guess as well," I confirmed. Terry, curiosity satisfied, jogged home. I grabbed Sam's leash and walked him around the front yard carefully stashing his old collar with that special charm in my purse for safe keeping.

Sam was so sweet I had to remind myself not to get attached. Once inside, I took Mazy's dish down from the kitchen cabinet thinking it seemed much too small for Sam, but I guess I could always give him seconds.

Sam must be hungry by now. I'm sure those Cheerios and treats at the vet's didn't cut it. He sniffed the air so he knew I brought in his food. I opened the bag of natural turkey kibbles with sweet potatoes and filled the small bowl. He looked at me I'm sure wondering if this was it before digging in. I did give him seconds and some ice water in one of my salad bowls.

I had a quick peanut butter and jelly sandwich. I was too tired to cook and my stomach churned the more I thought about calling the number on that bone shaped charm. Should I call tonight? Feeling like I had been through enough today, I remembered what my very wise mother told me. "Sometimes it's better to sleep on a problem, before rushing into action."

In this case, I thought Mom was right. It was ten o'clock so I went into my spare bedroom and grabbed a clean soft quilt. Sam followed me into my room and watched me spread the quilt on the floor before placing two small dog biscuits on it so he would know it was all right for him to sleep there. He dropped down on the quilt and rubbed his face in its softness before dozing off, too tired to eat his treats. Closing my bedroom door, I watched him sleep thinking about calling that number tomorrow and what I would find out.

Loud knocking and Sam's barking woke me from a sound sleep. Grabbing my purple silk kimono, I went to the kitchen door to find Sam facing it wagging his tail in excitement. I pushed the lace curtain on the door's window aside to see Terry in a very bright green and blue Hawaiian shirt trying to balance an armload of grocery bags. His arms were so full, it was amazing he could even free one hand to knock.

I unlocked the door and let him in as Sam pranced around in circles. I guess they bonded yesterday. Terry started to tease me.

"Wish I could be an editor and hang out until 10:30 in my kimono. You should be ashamed to call that work." He added with a wink. "Let me by please. I brought valuable supplies for humans and dog."

He barreled his way into my kitchen and placed the two large paper grocery bags on my counter. Sam, his nose in the air trying to get a sniff of the bags' contents, was hot on his heels. Terry pulled each item from the bags one by one like a magician. "Aha!" he exclaimed. "First we have a box of sweet potato dog treats."

He held the box low enough for Sam to get a whiff. "What's this? Here's a bag of chicken biscuits, rawhide chews and a new big dog dish. Mazy's old dish is nice but doesn't cut it."

Sam showed his approval by a long messy drool falling from the sides of his mouth. Terry's green eyes looked mischievous as he rattled something in the bag with jingle bells. Sam's ears picked straight up as my wonderful but sometimes crazy neighbor held up a collar made of plastic Christmas greens with red jingle bells. "Sam this is to get you in the Christmas spirit." He placed the collar around Sam's neck and the dog shook his head incessantly. I tried to be tactful about my next comment.

"Terry it's not that I'm not grateful for all of this but we haven't had our breakfast or coffee yet and I don't know how long I can listen to jingle bells."

My thoughtful neighbor smiled. "Got it. Sam let's go for a morning jog. If Jessica looks in the bag, she'll find some fresh honey dipped doughnuts with red and green sprinkles that will go perfectly with your collar and our morning coffee."

Our coffee? It's hard not to love this guy. He treats me like his little sister. As they left for a jog with Sam on Jeff's donated leash, I made coffee and found my holiday mugs, plastic plates, and paper napkins. Might as well keep this good cheer going. Who knows how I'll feel after I call the number on that charm?

Sam and Terry returned looking much too happy. "Sam met a lot of the neighbors. Of course I told them you were just dog sitting but they all loved him and offered to spend time with him when you need a break."

That's just great, I thought. He's become a local celebrity and I still don't even know who his owner is. I took off Sam's jingle bells, washed his new red dish, and filled it with the vet's food. Sam loved every morsel of it. I poured our coffee while Terry opened the box of delicious smelling doughnuts and placed one on each of my red plates. Like Sam, I sniffed the air drooling.

After Terry munched his doughnut and gulped his coffee, he told me. "Great Job Jess. We're celebrating the holiday already. On no! Look at the time. It's 11:30. Have a tennis lesson at noon. Love you both. See you soon." With that, he got up and exited in the same whirlwind in which he entered. Sam finished his food and drank some more water. I stroked his back knowing I shouldn't wait any longer to make that phone call. Since no one on the other end will see me, I didn't want to waste time changing. This job was too important.

I gave Sam one of the large rawhide bones Terry brought and went into my living room and sat at my desk. My purse was on my desk so I pulled out the torn collar with the charm and read the inscription.

"His name is Sam. If he's lost or hurt and you find him, please call 239-212-6457 Collect if necessary."

Even a travel editor like me could afford a local call. I picked up my cell and dialed the number. A tape recorded message answered. "You have reached the home number of Trey Musgrove of the law firm Musgrove and Garner. If I gave you this number for emergency reasons, I am either away from home or busy with another client, please contact my office at 239-212-6678 or leave a message after the beep."

My hands shook. My mind raced with questions. Should I leave a message? What kind of emergency calls does this attorney handle? Suppose he doesn't want Sam anymore, but why then leave a contact number? Leaving a cold recorded message will not do. I needed to speak to someone in person. I waited about ten minutes and called back hoping he would answer, but still had to listen to the same recording with the same results. This time, I wrote down his office number and decided to call it. By now, I had to find out how Sam got lost.

I glanced down at that beautiful gentle dog. He lay by my feet still chewing his rawhide, and, from the looks of it, content to do so. I took a deep breath to garner courage and dialed the office number on the recording. A sweet female voice answered. "Musgrove and Garner attorneys at law, this is Angelica speaking, how may I help you?"

My heart raced. I hesitated for a minute to regain my composure. More than a bit nervous, I asked. "May I please speak with Mr. Musgrove?"

Angelica responded at once. "Mr. Musgrove is out of the office temporarily. Would you like to speak to his partner Mr. Garner?"

I paused, "No. This is in regards to a personal matter."

Angelica advised. "Every call is personal to us and will remain as such. Are you hurt? Are you in a safe place?"

Why would she ask me questions like that? Cautious, I answered, "I'm going to have to think about this and call back."

"Please be careful. We're here to help when you need us."

I thanked her and hung up. That entire conversation seemed strange to me. How can I find out anything about this Musgrove guy? Since I was already at my desk, I opened my laptop. Google. That's it. I'll Google him. I entered "Trey Musgrove Florida Attorney".

Sure enough, after I did, a plethora of information opened up. First I saw his work bio, office address, even some of the high-profile divorce cases he handled. I understood now why Angelica asked if I was hurt and in a safe place. He's a divorce attorney.

CHAPTER 3

S am finished his chewy, sat up, and put his head on my lap.
I petted him. For a big dog, he's very clingy, more than
likely unsure of his new surroundings so he doesn't want to
lose sight of me. Keeping one hand on his head, I went back
to reading about Trey Musgrove. I found a headline and news
clip from our daily paper about him dated about one week
ago. The headline read, "Divorce Attorney T. Musgrove
involved in head-on collision." I clicked on the article to read
further. "Local attorney Trey Musgrove, 37, was hospitalized
last night for severe injuries resulting from a head-on collision
on Beach Road about one mile from the south bridge to
Hibiscus Island. The accident occurred at about eleven p.m.
on the single lane road."

I gasped. "My poor Sam. There are coyotes living in the
woods off of that road. What if they found him?" I continued
reading.

"The driver of the other car, Ned Frith, was arrested for
driving under the influence and taken to the county jail. The
sheriff's deputy on duty stated, 'The back door to Musgrove's
vehicle was bent and must have popped open before the
vehicle landed on its side. We don't know if there was a

passenger with him at the time of the accident and if he or she was hurt. If anyone has any information, please call us at the Lee County Sheriff's Department. 239-221-6655.'"

There was a color photo of Musgrove next to the article. I studied it. He was handsome, had a nice smile, and kind deep blue eyes. Sam must have been riding in the back seat and more than likely tore his collar and harness trying to escape. The accident happened over a week ago. No wonder Sam was in such bad shape. I gave him another pat. He loved it and wagged his tail as I read on.

"Musgrove was taken to Healthwell Hospital in South Ft. Myers in serious condition. As of this printing he remains stable there."

Wow! I looked at Sam, "I'm so happy. We may have found your Daddy." I can't lie, I'd like Sam to stay with me a bit longer, but I realized it was my responsibility to call his owner. After reading this article, I was sure he must be worried sick about his little boy. By now, I was too distracted to change. If anyone stops by I'll make up some lame excuse for my sloppy appearance. I am a writer after all. I looked up the number for Healthwell on my computer. My hands trembling, I took one more deep breath, and dialed the number hoping to get some resolve for Sam.

After two rings, the hospital switchboard picked up. "Healthwell Hospital. How may I direct your call?"

I answered in a strong confidant voice. "Mr. Trey Musgrove's room please."

That request led to an awkward pause before the operator responded. "I cannot give out that number, but I will connect you to his floor and have you speak with a nurse there."

"Thank you. I'd appreciate that," I answered. The receptionist then advised me. "I'll have to put you on hold for a few minutes but don't hang up. That floor is very busy, and it may take a while for them to pick up."

"I won't." I wondered why his floor was so busy. Finally, I

heard a click as a woman's voice answered.

"ICU. Nurse Andrews speaking. How may I help you?"

I responded. "I'd like to speak with Trey Musgrove please about a personal matter."

The nurse asked, "Please give me your name so I may check it against the approved contact list of relatives and friends."

I hedged. No matter how good a storyteller I was, there's no getting around her list. "I'm not on that list. I have his pet, and I'm concerned about his welfare."

Nurse Andrews then said, "Mr. Musgrove is unable to speak with anyone right now. I can't even tell you when to call back."

Why, I wondered. He must really be in bad shape, but for Sam's sake, I didn't let up. "I have an important message I need to get to him about his dog. It might make him feel better."

Nurse Andrews remained silent but after a sigh advised, "We're so busy, I can't guarantee the delivery of a verbal message, but if you can come up to ICU and give me a note with all the information in it, I'll personally make sure he reads it when he is able. Please give me your name and what time you think you'll be arriving. I'll let the information desk know you will be visiting me. I know how important pets are, especially Sam."

Sam? I didn't expect that. How does she know Sam?

She continued, "I know Sam because Mr. Musgrove was my divorce attorney. He helped get me out of an abusive relationship. I was broken emotionally and physically, and he found the professional care I needed to mend my mind and heart. He always had a photo of Sam on his desk and changed the photo often. Mr. Musgrove just loves that dog and often talked about his puppy antics. Now that he's hurt, it's my turn to return the favor and help him heal as best I can."

What a nice lady! I hit the jackpot with her. "I don't know if I can get there until four this afternoon. Will you be there?" I asked.

"Yes," she responded. "My shift ends at six. See you at four."

"See you then and thank you very much."

As soon as I hung up, I knew I had to find someone to watch Sam. I called his new best bud Terry and left a message on his machine. "I need your help. Can you please come over at three this afternoon and watch Sam for about two hours. I may have located Sam's owner but the poor guy's in bad shape. There's take-out Chinese in it for you and Rich. I'll pick up all your favorites on my way home from the hospital. Please call me back as soon as you get this message. Thanks. You're the best. Jess."

My stomach churned hoping he'll get my message. In the meantime I put the Christmas mugs in the dishwasher and threw away the paper plates and utensils before heading to my room to change with Sam following me. I carried my cell wishing it to ring on command like the phones in all those sci-fi movies do.

I stared at my cell before I yelled. "Ring, darn it, ring!" Sam looked up at me puzzled. He's never seen me this upset. I looked in my closet. What to wear? I haven't been to Healthwell since I used to meet Jake, my ex and a doctor, there after his shift. Oh my gosh! I almost forgot. He still works there. Just hope I don't run into him, especially since we had such an unfriendly break-up.

Wanting to make a good impression for Sam's sake, not to mention I found Mr. Musgrove's photo attractive, I picked out a navy blue skirt and pink silk blouse from my closet. Once dressed, I started to work on my face. After looking in the mirror, I wondered if I had enough time and enough make-up to fix it. Sam sat next to me enthralled by my make-up procedure.

I knew I had to get Mr. Musgrove's attention. Maybe a gift might help. Sam and I went into the living room. I put his Christmas collar on and told him to sit next to the tree. *Click Click Click.* When I checked my camera, I had taken ten candid photos in order to get one good enough to print. Animals are not the easiest of subjects. Sam did look extra adorable in one, so I downloaded it to my computer and printed out an eight by ten. Not as professional as the photo shop but still adorable. I remembered I had a framed eight by ten photo of Jake face down in my desk drawer so I took out that louse's photo and inserted Sam's. This was a much better use of that frame. I hope Mr. Musgrove will get a smile out of this photo. I then typed and printed my note for Nurse Andrews to give him.

Dear Mr. Musgrove,

I wanted you to know I found your dog, Sam, wandering around my yard, lost, yesterday. I took him to my vet, and she said he was fine just very hungry from probably not eating much for a week. She had him groomed and gave me food for him while my neighbor came by with treats. As you can see from this photo I took today, he is doing just fine. When you are ready, please contact me, Jessica Munroe at 239- 313-8878. He'll be well cared for until you're ready to take him home. He's no trouble and a really great dog. Please get better. Jessica and Sam.

I placed the note in an envelope and just as I was ready to put the photo and note in my huge bag, the phone rang. "Hey Jess, It's Terry. What's up?"

A deep sigh of relief came over me. "Oh thank goodness

you called. I think I may have found Sam's owner but he's in Healthwell Hospital. The head nurse in ICU said if I would bring her a written note about Sam, she would give it to his owner to read as soon as he was able. I can't visit him because my name isn't on his list of relatives and approved friends."

Terry uttered, "Huh. You sure you want to do this? Jake still works there, and you could open sore wounds. Besides do you want to let Sam go so soon? You two are a good match."

Of course I didn't want to lose Sam but knew it was the right thing to do. "I know the pitfalls. But this guy may be worrying himself sick about Sam, thinking he was the cause of his dog's distress. I'm sure just knowing Sam's safe may help him heal faster. As for Jake, I lost any and all feelings for that excuse for a man. Don't worry. I won't let Jake ruin my life any more ever again. So can you please come at three and watch Sam? I promise I'll bring home take-out from Chang's so invite Rich to join us."

Terry's voice sounded happy. "I can and will. It'll be fun to stay with Sam. He's like a grand dog. I can play with him when I want and leave all the doggie duties to you. Anyway, I appreciate your dinner offer, but I can cook for us."

"Thanks, but you both are always so good to me I'd like to do this for you."

"Okay. I'll tell Rich. See you at three."

I felt so lucky. Terry and his partner, Rich, were the best neighbors in the world. They moved in five years ago. Both men in their sixties, they had traveled the world after retiring from professional careers. Terry was an accountant; Richard an architect. They moved to Hibiscus Island, because they wanted our laid-back island lifestyle. I'm so thankful they chose to buy the house next door to me.

We hung up. Sam and I went into the kitchen to take off Sam's holiday collar and fill his salad bowl with water. I held up his leash. "Ready for your walk, buddy?"

He panted and wagged a "yes" so out we went for a walk

around the front yard to get ready for Terry. Three o'clock on the dot I heard a knock on the front door.

"Terry here, reporting for Sam duty."

I opened the door and Sam jumped up to greet him with a wet slurpy kiss. Terry had to fight his way in. When they settled down, I picked up my purse.

"Wish me luck, boys."

"Always," Terry responded with a smile. I left and locked the front door wondering who and what information awaited me at Healthwell Hospital.

I sat in my car ready to drive off when my cell buzzed. I looked at the number "Unknown." Probably a sales call. I usually don't take a chance, but with all the unusual stuff going on, I decided to answer.

"Hello."

"Jess, this is Nurse Andrews. I'm calling from my cell. We spoke earlier about your visit at four. As I explained, your name could not be added to any visitor list, but since I knew how important Sam was to Mr. Musgrove, I called down to visitor registration and told them I was waiting for a visitor named Jessica Munroe who was expected to arrive at four. I asked the receptionist to give you a visitor's badge not for any specific room or patient but one so you could come see me directly at the nurses' station in ICU."

That was a surprise, a very nice one at that. "Thank you so much," I replied. "I appreciate your help and I'm sure Sam will as well. I'm about to leave for the hospital now. I don't like to be late for appointments. I'll see you a little before four."

"Wonderful dear, See you then."

We hung up and I started to drive to Healthwell. Along the way, I made a quick detour to Buzzy's Farm Market, the only outdoor market on our island, to buy a large pot of red poinsettias. Purchase complete, I drove back to the main road. The traffic was terrible, probably due to holiday shoppers, so my trip took a bit longer than expected to get to the hospital, but I still arrived there at three forty-five. I walked in the main entrance and over to the visitor registration desk. An elderly volunteer with blue gray hair wearing a blue pin striped uniform opened the glass window.

"How may I assist you?" she asked in a pleasant voice.

"My name is Jessica Munroe and I'm here for an appointment with Nurse Andrews in ICU."

"Ah yes," she responded. "She notified us ahead of your arrival. Now all I need from you is a photo ID, preferably your driver's license."

I opened my large red leather bag I use for a purse and found my wallet. I gave her my license. She scanned it into her computer before printing out a stick-on badge with my photo on it. She handed me the badge through the open window adding, "Please wear this the entire time you're in the hospital. You'll find Nurse Andrews on the sixth floor in the ICU. Lovely holiday flowers. You do know many of our patients in ICU cannot have any flowers in their room."

I nodded that I knew. "They're for the nurses' station. Hopefully I can bring them a little holiday cheer."

I took a quick look at my enlarged license photo. Maybe I should have given her another form of ID with a better photo. Since she already told me where to find ICU, I turned around and walked to the elevators' stainless steel doors and pushed the up button. One opened and who should walk out with a group of doctors but Jake my ex. Just my luck. He appeared much happier to see me than I was to see him as he took me aside.

"Hey, Jess. How are you doing? You look great. Again sorry about our break-up but I just couldn't lie to you anymore."

CHAPTER 4

I scowled. "Whatever. I can't talk about that now because I have a meeting at four." I pushed Jake aside and went back to the elevators to push that up button again before adding, "Take good care of yourself, Jake, and that new squeeze of yours."

I can't lie. Boy, did that feel good! Once in the elevator, I pushed the sixth-floor button as fast as I could. When I arrived in the ICU, I walked by rooms filled with patients, some lucid some not, to head toward the nurses' station. Those worrisome scenes were in deep contrast to a small white Christmas tree with red decorations at the nurses' station. A tall thin nurse in a starched white uniform bearing a name badge stood and waved me over. She appeared to be in her sixties with brown hair salted with gray. She spoke to me in a soothing voice.

"You must be Jessica. I'm Nurse Andrews. It's very nice to meet you. Now what did you bring me for Mr. Musgrove to see? You know he can't have any flowers."

I smiled. "I know. These are for the nurses' station. You all work so tirelessly. I can't even imagine how difficult it must be to work with such sick patients and away from your family over the holidays."

Nurse Andrews, tears forming in the corners of her blue eyes, took the potted plant. "How thoughtful of you. Thank you for the flowers and for your kind thoughts. I'm going to place them right here on the counter next to our tree so anyone getting off the elevator will see them. Now what did you bring for my patient?"

I opened my big bag and pulled out my framed holiday photo of Sam. "I took this today. I thought if Mr. Musgrove saw how happy Sam is, it might cheer him up and make him feel better."

Nurse Andrews remained silent. Then I took out the envelope addressed to Mr. Musgrove that contained my note.

"Please give him this note when he's ready. It's about how and where I found Sam and how I've been taking care of him so Mr. Musgrove wouldn't worry about him."

Nurse Andrews took my note and as she finished reading it, an odd look came across her face. "Jessica, I don't want to lie to you or get your hopes up. Sam may be with you for a long time."

She came out from the nurse's station and took me aside.

"I probably shouldn't tell you this, but I will since no one else in his life seems to care about visiting him. Mr. Musgrove suffered a serious head injury during a head-on auto accident. He's incurred some swelling on his brain and is in a medically induced coma to try to reduce that swelling. What a shame. He's young, in his thirties, successful, and ever since our first meeting in his office, I thought kind and very handsome."

I was stunned. For some reason, I didn't expect to hear about the severity of his condition. Surprised she said no one cared enough to visit him, I had to ask, "Doesn't he have a wife or other family members who love him?"

Nurse Andrews shook her head negative. "He's not married, and his immediate relatives have been notified. So far no one has showed up. I doubt if his doctor will give any medical information to someone not on the approved list. I've been told his parents, now retired, do missionary work all over the globe. They have been advised and decided not to come home. At the moment they're in Africa but do stay in constant touch with Trey's doctors. They are quite well off and made sure he had the top three US specialists for brain trauma available for consultation."

Nurse Andrews checked the nurses' station to see if she was needed before continuing. "I remember Trey told me he had one sister, a workaholic high end fashion designer in New York City. When notified, she told his doctor on staff here that she couldn't take time off from her work for Trey's stupid accident. Imagine not wanting to take time off for a sick relative? I've known Trey for a while and she sure did not inherit his caring genes. To be honest, you are his first and only visitor since the accident except of course for his law partner and insurance adjustors who took photos of him and asked for photocopies of his charts, I'm sure for a likely lawsuit. The Musgrove name is pretty prevalent in this area. His family has done so much for the community. His great grandfather, Franklin Musgrove, made loads of money in the Florida sugar industry and donated to a variety of causes. That's why you see the Musgrove name on so many parks and buildings even this hospital has the Franklin Musgrove Wing for Cardiac Care." My lips quivered. I felt so sad for Mr. Musgrove's lack of family support and love.

"I'm very sorry to hear he's alone during this trauma. When he's out of the coma, will you read my note to him? It's for Sam's benefit. He's fine and can stay with me for as long as necessary. When Mr. Musgrove wakes up, maybe I could bring Sam to the hospital property and we could stand under his window."

The good nurse shrugged her shoulders. "My dear, you are so sweet. I don't know if he'll wake up or when and even then if he'll know what's going on once he does. Those are all big if's. Like I said his injury was severe."

I don't even know the man and Nurse Andrews' information brought tears to my eyes. "Please promise to call me when he comes out of the coma. I have to think positive thoughts for his recovery."

Nurse Andrews touched my hand. "Jessica, you are a very caring person. Everyone could use a guardian angel like you. I will place Sam's photo on his nightstand and promise to read him the note as soon as he wakes up. Thank you for coming. Most people would have sent Sam to the shelter. Thanks for that as well. I know how much Mr. Musgrove loves him."

I squeezed her hand thanking her for her help and left wishing Mr. Musgrove a complete recovery.

I woke up this morning excited. Today, the first Sunday in December, the island celebrates Christmas with a holiday boat parade. I was invited to ride on my neighbor Hal's pontoon boat since I helped him decorate it the day before Thanksgiving, two days before Sam's arrival.

We made a huge snowman out of different size Styrofoam balls, painted a happy expression on his face, and dressed him in one of Jake's old holiday T-shirts that read "Beach Frosty" with Santa holding a frosted mug on the front. We gave our snowman a fishing cap and pole with a rubber fish dangling from its hook. Since Hal was a fisherman himself, he loved it.

In his eighties, a widower, and very kind, Hal offered Sam a ride as well. I knew Sam was all right with people, but since Hal always took Coco, his small mixed breed lap dog, on his boat, I called Hal and declined explaining I wasn't sure if Sam and Coco would become friends or if Coco would end up Sam's lunch. Hal laughed and thanked me again for helping. I knew he appreciated my assistance since he lived alone losing his wife to cancer three years ago.

Sam and I could still watch the parade from the bridge on the south end of the island. I fed Sam and ate breakfast, showered, and put on shorts and my Mrs. Claus T-shirt. Of course Sam wore his jingle collar.

I squeezed Sam into the backseat of my Mini Cooper and drove to that small bridge. We parked on a side street nearby and walked onto the bridge standing over where the boat parade starts. The decorated boats will line up and pass under us before heading into the Back Bay, and on to the marina in the center of the island where the parade ends. Everyone on the bridge was there to cheer their favorite entry. Awards await the best decorated boats at the marina as well as refreshments. It would be great if "we" won one. The minute the first boat passed under the bridge my cell buzzed. "Unknown" appeared on my screen but I now could recognize the number as Nurse Andrews. I turned away from the noise, plugged my ear with my free hand while my other hand held onto Sam's leash, and answered. "Yes."

I heard a familiar woman's voice respond. "Jessica? This is Starra Andrews, you know, Nurse Andrews. I wanted to give you an update on Mr. Musgrove. He moved his right hand even while under the anesthesia."

"Anesthesia?"

Starra answered. "Yes. Doctors use anesthesia to medically induce a coma. Different kinds, of course, for different brain diagnoses. Mr. Musgrove's doctor informed me earlier this morning that since he's seen constant improvements, he may bring him out of the coma early next week. Even then, Trey will need time and treatment to get back to normal. Please keep your fingers crossed. As I said before, I shouldn't be telling you this, but you care for Sam and appear to sympathize with Trey. Oh and if you're wondering about my first name. My mother named me that because I was born during a meteor shower. Please call me Starra."

I smiled. "That's a lovely name. Thank you for calling with that information, Starra. Sam and I appreciate it. Have a great Sunday."

I turned around to face the parade. Bystanders waved to the crews of their favorite entries. It seemed like there were more boats than last year all with wonderfully creative decorations. A mermaid angel, a Santa Shrimp, even twelve fishermen dressed like reindeer with Santa on the roof of their boat. This event has always been so much fun. I looked down at my newfound buddy who barked at all these strange sights but wagged his tail and seemed to love it as much as I did. I mentally wished Mr. Musgrove a speedy recovery but knew I would sure miss Sam after that happened.

Parade finished, I turned when I heard familiar voices. Terry and Rich, in bright colored surfer jams and matching T's, were leaving for the holiday bar-b-que in the town park that always followed the parade. Everyone including well behaved pets was welcome to attend.

"Hey, Jess, follow us to the bar-b-que. All the winners will be announced there again."

I nodded before Sam and I went back to my car. The traffic to the park on the other side of the island was thick, slow, and bumper to bumper. When we finally made it to the park, I found a parking space on a side street, and we went off to look for Terry and Rich. I couldn't find them but did notice Dr. Evil standing there with his new blonde bimbo.

Jake, wearing lime green surfer jams, waved. "Hey, Jess. Who's this? Got a new dog? Sorry to hear about Mazy. She was a good dog. Anyway, come over to meet Barbie. She's a nurse at Healthwell. Barbie this is Jess, my ex."

Now this was as awkward as it could be. What am I supposed to say? "Nice to meet you Mrs. Evil" or maybe "You two make such a cute couple. I'm so glad Jake dumped me" or perhaps "Barbie, what an appropriate name for eye candy, just like the doll."

As those thoughts crossed my mind, I just answered a reluctant, "Hi."

Luckily, Barbie in a tiny red bikini with a sheer white net cover-up was more interested in Sam than me. "He's really cute for a big dog. What's his name? Does he bite?"

Right now I wished he did. "No, Sam does not bite." I answered politely. Barbie leaned over to pet him, but Sam backed away and growled a low growl like he was trying to warn me. I've read dogs are the best judge of character. They can sense their owner's feelings about other people. He sure sensed mine. "I'm sorry, Barbie. I don't know what's come over him. Maybe being in the center of all these people is unsettling for him."

She backed off. "That's okay. Maybe another time, but I could swear I've seen him before."

How could that be unless she dated Mr. Musgrove before Jake? I suppose that was possible. As if a lightbulb lit in her brain, she blurted out. "Now I remember. One of my ICU patients had a photo of a dog like yours on his nightstand. What breed is Sam?"

I didn't want to answer "mixed" since she would know that picture was of him. So I made a breed up. "He's a Golden German, although rare and from Germany, there are some found locally."

"Wow, that's so cool," is all Barbie could answer. I don't think Jake accepted the made-up breed name as easily. "And where did you get this Golden German?"

"From a new friend. I do make friends you know."

"Is your new friend male or female?" he persevered.

"What difference does that make? Oh, look! Here come Terry and Rich. *Au revoir, Mon Amis*. Have fun."

"Not so fast, Jess. I had a patient in the emergency room last week with a brain trauma. I sent him to ICU. The only words he said before going up to ICU were 'Find Sam.' Lucky I sent him up there. The specialist placed him in a medically induced coma which might have saved his life. Now Barbie sees a photo of a dog that looks like Sam. So tell me again where did Sam come from?"

How in my wildest dreams could I have imagined that Jake took care of Mr. Musgrove when he was rushed into the emergency room? How can I hate Jake that much when he does so much good? I guess it's because he does it for everyone else but me. Since he played medical detective every day, I might as well come clean.

"I am taking care of Sam for your patient, Mr. Musgrove. Evidently Sam escaped from his car after the accident and wandered around for quite a few days until he ended up in my front yard. He was dirty, emaciated, and dehydrated. My story is all on the up and up. Nurse Andrews knows I have him and will take good care of him until Mr. Musgrove regains consciousness and is able to go home. You should have seen how bad Sam looked when he found me. He was dirty, thin, and confused at being lost I'm sure. Sam's been to my vet, groomed, and eats like a little piggy. I just couldn't send him to the county shelter. After all, it's Christmas."

Jake actually smiled at me. "Jess, I forgot what a big heart you have. You're doing a wonderful thing for Sam and Musgrove, but please be careful. I know how much you love animals. When you volunteered at the shelter, I remember you telling me you wanted to take them all home. Please don't get too attached. It will be that much harder to give Sam back."

Barbie came over and gave me a big hug. "You are such a caring person. As a nurse, I appreciate what you're doing for Sam and my patient."

That remark almost made me want to take back my petty mental remarks about her.

Jake then added, "Listen, taking care of a young guy like

Sam can get expensive especially for an associate editor. If we can help you in any way with food or vet bills, just call."

Who thought a dog could make peace although brief between two warring factions like Jake and me. I tried to hide my tears. "Thanks, Jake and Barbie. I appreciate that offer more than you know. Terry helped and so did Mazy's vet. Barbie did see Sam's photo on her patient's night table. I brought it in to Nurse Andrews along with a note about Sam's location and his care. Sam is not a Golden German. He's a mixed breed with German Shepherd and Golden Lab, but I think he's just beautiful."

Barbie smiled. "I do too, honey, and so are you. Jake has your number so if there are any significant changes with my patient, I'll let you know."

Feeling someone touching my shoulder, I turned to see Terry with Rich standing behind me. "Hey, Jess. There you are. We thought you got lost. Ready to eat bar-b-que?"

Sam heard the word "eat" and wagged his tail like crazy. We all laughed. I nodded and Terry, Rich, and I followed Sam with his extra sensitive dog nose in the air to that delicious smelling cook-out. He had us walking so fast, we left a trail of sand in the air behind us.

CHAPTER 5

Three days passed since the bar-b-que and my unexpected meeting with Barbie and Jake. Whoever dreamed a dog could get us to briefly stop bickering just in time for Christmas?

Every year I open my cottage on Christmas Eve to welcome anyone with nowhere to go for Christmas and no one to celebrate the holiday. About sixty or so people stop by for what has become an island holiday tradition. Most bring a dish to share. As they leave, I give each guest a small wrapped gift hoping it won't be their only one.

I plan ahead and buy small items for this event throughout the year. I finished getting my holiday cards ready to e-mail and needed to buy gift wrap, tags, and tape. I thought I would stop by Island Hardware which was more like an old-fashioned general store. I looked at Sam. He was content to chew his bone so I tried to pick up my car keys from the front hall table as quietly and quickly as I could hoping he wouldn't hear me. I'd call Terry on my way to check in on him.

Oops. That didn't work. His floppy ears stood up straight and the next thing I knew he was standing by my side wagging his tail ready to go for a ride. What do I do now? I guess take him to the store with me. I fastened his leash and off we went.

Decorated for the holidays with silver and gold garlands, Island Hardware had a sign on its front door. "Well behaved leashed pets are always welcome. The others will be sent to The Grinch."

As Sam and I entered, the store's overdone holiday cheer made me smile. Paper cut-outs of Santas, snowmen, and snowflakes handmade by Beach School students hung from the ceiling panels. For some reason, maybe it's our warm weather or that we have no snow, everything in Florida gets over decorated for Christmas. On the bright side, however, we do have beautiful beach weather.

Joe, who's owned the store for as long as I can remember, was at the counter wearing a red Santa hat to cover his bald head and a pink flowered Hawaiian shirt. He was surprised by my new companion.

"Well, who's your new friend? New pet, Jess? He's a big dog for your size."

I sighed. "No. No more pets after I lost my Mazy. Her passing broke my heart. Anyway I'd like to introduce you to Sam. I'm taking care of him until his owner gets out of the hospital."

"You're always someone's guardian angel, aren't you? That's really nice. Can I help you find anything?"

I gave him a mischievous look. "Well, I need wrapping stuff. Would you mind if I left Sam with you while I run back and grab some. The aisles are so jam packed, I'm afraid he'll knock something over."

Joe looked into Sam's puppy dog eyes. "No problem, you know I'm a big dog person."

I left Sam to charm Joe and picked up two rolls of red and green paper and one of gold and silver, some pretty gift tags, and clear tape. I returned to the counter with my arms full ready to check out only to see Joe petting Sam while feeding him treats.

"You two made friends fast. You do know, I'll never get him to go home with me now."

Joe laughed. "I opened the box to give him a couple. These were my Ringo's favorites. Sam loves these cookies so much I'm sending the rest of the box home with him. No charge as long as you promise to please bring him back to visit me. I miss Ringo, you remember him, my Golden Retriever, but I'm too old to get another dog especially a big one like Ringo or Sam."

I thanked Joe, paid my bill before taking my gift wrap supplies and Sam with his new box of cookies to my car. Right after we got settled, my cell buzzed. I looked at the number "Healthwell Hospital."

I answered, surprised to hear a very perky voice on the other end of the line. "Hey, Jess, Barbie here. Nurse Andrews has the day off so I'm calling you from ICU to tell you Mr. Musgrove blinked his eyes. His specialist now feels he is a candidate to come out of the coma by the end of this week. They want to monitor his progress a little further. Nurse Andrews will more than likely call you tomorrow. Please don't mention my call. I'm not supposed to do this, but you are so kind to Sam and so concerned about my patient that I really want to help. We both want to help you and Sam. Jake is dropping off some large bags of natural dog food early this evening after his shift. Don't be too harsh on him. Your break-up was half my fault. We fell hard for each other. Oops a lab tech is headed to my desk. I'll call back when I can."

Click. She hung up. Wow! Trey Musgrove blinked his eyes. I hugged my new best guy saying. "Hey, Sam you might see your Daddy soon."

Sam wagged his tail. I don't know if he understood me or by the tone of my voice realized I was happy. I started the car and drove him home all the way trying to keep him from breaking into that new box of cookies.

When we arrived home, I let him out so I could carry my purchases inside. Sam ran straight to the front door like he's always lived here. I opened the front door for him and dropped off my purchases in the living room.

I looked up at my wall clock. Five-fifteen. Sam will need a walk before dinner. I like to wait until dusk because my neighbors have their holiday lights lit by then, plus I can see their Christmas trees through their front windows.

Sam and I went back outside for our walk when a fancy black jaguar convertible pulled up. It was Jake. I'll try not to be too hard on him since he was trying to help out with Sam. He parked and pulled out two massive bags of dry gourmet dog food from the passenger seat.

"I can take them inside if you like. They're pretty heavy. I didn't want you and this wonderful dog to run out of supplies too soon."

Sam liked him and pulled me over to Jake to get petted. I don't know if Jake could feel how much my heart ached for him right now, but I had to remain stoic for Sam's sake. "Thanks for your help and for all the food, Jake. I appreciate this more than you know."

I unlocked my front door and Jake carried the bags inside and put them in my pantry closet. It hasn't been that long since we were together so I'm not surprised he remembered his way around.

Turning to leave, Jake gave me a funny look. "You know, Jess, even if they bring Mr. Musgrove out of the coma, he can't go straight home. He will be weak, may experience some degree of muscle atrophy, and will need the care of a rehab center. Sam could be with you until Christmas, maybe even longer. That's why I bought such big bags. I'm sorry about us. You were always sweet and kind to me. You're a treasure some lucky man will discover. I love you like a friend and always will. Remember, I'm always here for you."

That brought tears to my eyes. I guess I should hate what he did and not who he was, but I'm still unable to do that. He left a piercing wound on my heart. As soon as Jake left, Sam and I went back outside to finish our walk with all those beautiful holiday lights leading our way. We had an early dinner before we watched my favorite Christmas movie "It's A Wonderful Life."

At the exact time the bell on the Christmas tree in the movie rang signifying an angel got her wings, my cell buzzed. I paused the movie to answer. Hope this will be an angel calling with more good news. I looked at the number. Not exactly the angel I hoped for. It was Barbie.

"Hey, girl. I know it's late, but I thought you might like to know, the doctors ran a few more tests on Mr. Musgrove and he's had some significant changes."

For some reason, I panicked. I held my breath hoping the changes were good ones. I remained silent as Barbie continued, "Jess, you still there?"

I answered, "Yes. I am."

She continued. "They tested him to see if he could follow an object like a pen with his eyes or turn his head on command. They think he's ready to come out of the coma and are going to prep him tomorrow. Please do not come until Nurse Andrews calls you. She approved of my call. I'm sure you'll get an update from one of us tomorrow."

With that good news, Barbie did become my angel ringing the bell on my Christmas tree. I gushed. "That's really great news, but I'll wait for a call to see how he is before coming to the hospital. Thanks for thinking of me and thanks for Sam's food."

We hung up. Sam sat right next to me panting. I think he sensed we received good news. I petted him and we finished our movie hoping for as good an ending to our predicament as the one in the movie.

I woke up the next morning to find Sam lying in bed next to me staring into my eyes. I shook myself wondering how such a big creature could find enough space in such a small double bed. I looked at my clock. Eight-thirty. Sam must be ready to go out. I threw on shorts and a T, grabbed his leash, and out the front door we went. Some of my neighbors who had never seen him before were curious. "That's quite a furry holiday present you got yourself," Mr. Edge laughed as he petted Sam's head.

I wanted to explain my dilemma but feared it would take too long. Still waiting to hear about Mr. Musgrove, I had to finish edits for my article, and bake cookies for the senior center.

I loved to bake for the center every year especially since the seniors enjoy my cookies so much. I will deliver them tomorrow for a late morning celebration. I wondered how difficult that might be this year because of Sam.

Back home, I fed Sam, but before I could put his water bowl on the floor, my cell rang. "Unknown." How boring my life must be if "Unknown" is my most frequent caller. Sam was chowing down on his food as I answered.

"Jess, Starra here. I called to let you know the doctors were successful in bringing Mr. M out of the coma. He is awake and aware and is resting comfortably. Later this afternoon we'll get him out of bed for a walk on this floor. Since you have been his only visitor, I had the doctor approve a visit for you tomorrow afternoon. Please let me know what time you'll be here. I have to remind you, you may have to take care of Sam for a while, perhaps a month. Please take care and call me back with a time."

Surprised, I answered. "I will. Thanks for calling with such great news." Excited and apprehensive, I asked myself, what if he doesn't want to see me or wanted me to leave Sam with someone in his office? Starra already said Musgrove was crazy about Sam so I think he'd be happy with my decision.

I had to calm down and think about something else. Cookies. That's it, my cookies. I should start on them right away. Since I plan for this every year, I had all of the ingredients on hand. I cleaned and cleared the kitchen table and found my other big bowl to mix dough, since Sam was using my only other one for water.

Sam became curious. Luckily my kitchen table was just a bit higher than his mouth. I got out my rolling pin and cookie baking sheets ready to start. I rolled out the dough to use the most important tools of all, my cookie cutters. They had belonged to my mother and were in the shapes of angels, bells, Santas, reindeer, and stars. I love Christmas cookies!

I had Sam's undivided attention as I pressed the different shaped cutters into the dough before arranging them on my cookie sheet. I had two large platters set aside for cooling my cookies as soon as they came out of the oven. Since I only have two cookie sheets I had to rotate their use arranging the dough shaped figures for every baking. I then found the pretty holiday tins I bought after Christmas last year. A writer has to be very careful with her money. I washed and dried them and let everything sit while Sam and I went into the other room to work on my article about traveling to Lapland over the holidays.

I worked on my column for about fifteen minutes before going back to finish the cookies. Now for the fun part! I made homemade vanilla frosting, divided it into small bowls, and added a different food coloring and flavor to each bowl. I started with the angels frosting them pink with white sparkles. I turned the Santa's red with multi-colored sparkles, the bells blue, the stars and reindeer yellow. I placed wax paper in the tins and when the frosting dried placed an assortment of cookies in each one. I soon had six deep tins ready for the senior center. I usually kept the small overflow for me, but this year, I thought Mr. Musgrove might enjoy some since his holiday season hasn't exactly gone as planned, so I wrapped and placed his in a small gift bag.

I left two cookies out for me to taste. They were as delicious as they looked. Sam lay by my feet drooling. He was so sweet I couldn't wait to take him to the senior center with me tomorrow. Once we returned home, I would grab the gift bag, and head straight to the hospital. I looked down at him, "Tomorrow honey, I'm going to meet your Daddy. Oh, my gosh! I have to call Starra with a time and Terry to play with you."

I called Nurse Andrews and set up an appointment for three. Needing to stop stressing about tomorrow, I took Sam out back for a quick round of fetch with his new Santa ball before returning to my article on Lapland. Sam followed me to my desk. He lay so close I could hardly turn my chair around but loved the fact he wanted to be with me.

I thought about my article which was about my own visit to Lapland. My parents were hippies in the 1960s. They always did unusual things and wanted their kids to follow suit. "Live your life today." They always advised me.

That made me remember the Christmas season when my sister Flower and I wanted to stay home to be in the Christmas pageant at our church; my parents, however, had other things in store for us. They decided we should have another "See the world" experience. I was ten and Flower eleven. Mom and Dad's planned adventure didn't sound as wonderful to us then as it might sound now at my age. Anyway, off to Lapland the four of us went. We spent our holiday with some rugged and beautiful people who took us on a sleigh ride pulled by reindeer. For a Florida kid, I saw the cleanest and most beautiful white snow and blue ice. Not to give myself a pat on the back, but I took some amazing photos. So much so that after I found them, I was able to scan them into my computer and use them in this article. Even at ten, I knew I wanted to be a writer.

I remembered how Sis and I used to get upset by these impromptu trips, but now I know how lucky I was to have visited places like Lapland, Machu Picchu, and Easter Island. Besides, I think some of that hippy spirit rubbed off on me. I don't exactly have a traditional lifestyle, but odd enough my sister Flower does. She married a strait-laced conservative accountant, has a lovely big house in the suburbs of Orlando and two beautiful children; a boy named Harry and a girl named Catherine.

Anyway, I was going through some old boxes after my parents died and found all of my photos from all of these amazing trips. I wrote this article from my heart about my personal journey with my family. Now I just need to polish the story and send it back to the travel magazine for print and distribution next week right in time for the holiday.

Working on my article kept my mind occupied for most of the afternoon. I completed all of my edits and e-mailed it off to my editor-in-chief. Once sent, I was relieved I finished by my deadline. I looked up at my wall clock. Wow. Where did my day go? It was five thirty, so I got Sam up and ready for our walk. He returned famished; I came back not hungry, with butterflies in my stomach, and worried about meeting Mr. Musgrove tomorrow.

I'd better call Terry about taking care of Sam tomorrow. I was so preoccupied with my article and the cookies I almost forgot. I heard him answer. "Hello, this is Terry, Jess' best friend. My lady, how may I be of service?"

He made me laugh. "Hey, guy, I need a big favor. I received a call from Mr. Musgrove's nurse that his medical team successfully brought him out of the coma. She said I could visit him tomorrow afternoon."

"Now that's the kind of good news we all need near Christmas. Of course I'll stay with my buddy. Don't know what we're all going to do when you have to give him back."

"I know we'll all miss him, but I have to give him back."

Terry changed the subject. "What time will you need me?"

"About two tomorrow afternoon. I made my appointment for three since I visit the senior center in the morning. Thanks, you're the best. See you tomorrow."

I went to bed that night wondering what that handsome Mr. M. was like and if he'll be happy to learn a total stranger like me has his dog.

I set my alarm for 6:00 a.m. I had such an exciting day ahead; I shouldn't waste one more second in bed. I was finally going to meet the handsome Mr. M. and loved hosting my yearly holiday visit to the senior center. My visits are always fun and by Sam accompanying me, this year will be more so. Good thing I called yesterday afternoon to see if they allowed pets. They did but will have to check his temperament upon arrival.

We raced through our morning routine. I placed his jingle bell collar around his neck while I was all set in my red and white Santa T, denim skirt, and Santa hat. I hurried to load the cookie tins in my car's front seat along with my small collapsible grocery cart. I put Sam on his leash and stuffed him into the back seat.

When we arrived at the center, I noticed their sign, "The Mathilda Musgrove Senior Center." Funny, all the times I've been here, I never noticed that. Nurse Andrews was right about the Musgroves.

I took out my grocery cart to unload the tins before grabbing Sam's leash. "Ready?" I asked him. So in we went ready to spread holiday cheer to others who have no family left or whose family is too far to visit. As soon as we entered, I took Sam aside to get him checked, not surprised he passed with flying colors. We went back into the main foyer to see all thirty participants, dressed in their best Christmas red and green, line up on chairs or stand with walkers to cheer us in. We walked under garlands of paper snowflakes made by Beach School kids and into their community room. The staff already had a long table covered with a holiday cloth and four large platters set out for my treats. They had paper plates and napkins with elves on them next to the platters.

There were pitchers of lemonade, iced tea, and carafes of coffee on the sideboard. I was so happy! I wanted to bring them cheer, but I think they brought me more than I could ever bring them. Susan, the director, helped unload my cart of cookie tins while I introduced myself and Sam to everyone.

"Hi. Merry Christmas. Most of you already know me, but for those who don't, my name is Jessica Munroe. I'm so thrilled to be here with you all again this year and spent most of yesterday baking. This year, I brought a new friend with me. This young man's name is Sam."

A woman from the audience interrupted me. "Jess we're so thrilled to have you here. We look forward to your visit every Christmas. After all, you are our Christmas angel."

The rest of the group applauded. Wow! I didn't expect that. Tears formed in my eyes as I continued. "Thank you so much. You all are my angels. As you can see by Sam's big tail wagging, he is happy to be here too. Anyone who would like to pet Sam please raise your hand and I'll walk him over to you."

So many hands went up, I couldn't count them all. There were claps and whispers as they watched Susan volunteer to approach Sam first. I told him to sit so Susan could let him sniff her hand before she gave him a giant bear hug. Everyone laughed. I walked Sam around the room and gave anyone who wanted a chance to meet him. While we were doing that, two kitchen staffers opened the tins and arranged the colorful treats on the platters. They then passed around hand sanitizer and elf napkins.

"We look forward to this every year. We just love it," an elderly lady with a walker said. "I'm not able to bake anymore, but I used to love to make Christmas cookies." Some "me toos" followed as they enjoyed my treats.

When everyone had their fill, Susan gave each senior a mini candy cane to decorate the tree in their front lobby. Cookies eaten, Sam petted, she and I led the group in a carol sing along. They all loved "Silent Night" so we sang that one twice.

Our two-hour party over, I walked around the room and gave each of them a hug. Sam waited with Susan. I had tears in my eyes seeing how grateful they were. I thought of my granny Meta who is no longer with me and how proud she would have been of me. I donated the tins for the center to store the leftover cookies and Sam and I left for home.

When we got in the car, I looked at my watch. Perfect. One forty-five. I can walk Sam, pick up the gift bag of cookies and go to the hospital. I looked at Sam like he was capable of advising me. "What do you think? Should I change or bring my holiday cheer into your daddy's room."

Sam's warm tongue went up and down my cheek. "Holiday cheer it is."

All the way to the hospital, my heart raced. The more I thought about how handsome Mr. Musgrove looked in that news photo, the more I couldn't wait to meet him.

I arrived at Healthwell, picked up my pre-arranged visitor's badge, and headed directly to the sixth floor. I was so curious about him I couldn't get there fast enough. Starra was on duty at the nurse's station. Her face lit up like the shooting stars that influenced her name when she saw me. She called out, "Jess, please hurry. I told Trey you were coming. He's anxious to meet you. Please follow me."

Starra walked briskly. I followed her pace into his room. Since I studied that photo online so many times, I felt like I already knew him. My heart pounded when I noticed the curtain surrounding his hospital bed was half closed. Starra walked us around to where he could see us, and we could see him before introducing me.

"Trey Musgrove, this is Jessica Munroe. She's the young woman who sent you the note about Sam."

Trey's gaze was turned away from me as he drank water from a straw held by another nurse. When he turned to face me, his blue eyes took mine hostage. My body trembled from his stare. It was as if we had known each other for a long time. He looked a bit paler and thinner than in that photo but still incredibly handsome. There should be a law against being that handsome. His kind blue eyes looked tired and he appeared weak like Jake said because he might have "atrophied muscles."

I remained quiet to let him speak first. He looked at me, well, really stared at me. I wondered if my holiday outfit was over the top. He spoke as I held up my holiday cookie bag.

"Jessica, I appreciate your visit and for taking such good care of my Sam. I can't tell you how relieved I felt after reading your note since I feared the worst after no one found him near the accident scene. I can tell by looking at you that's he's a very lucky dog."

His deep voice was weak but sexy. He shot me a smile as he continued. "I love your Christmas spirit."

CHAPTER 6

That made me smile. For some odd reason, perhaps because I studied his photo so many times, I felt comfortable with him.

"Trey," Nurse Andrews asked, "will you be all right if I left you alone with your visitor or would you like me to stay?"

Trey replied quickly, "I'm fine being alone with Jess. Who wouldn't be with such a pretty woman?"

I blushed as I asked Starra before she left us. "I baked some holiday cookies for the Island Senior Center yesterday and delivered them this morning. I left some out for Mr. Musgrove. Is it all right for him to have some?"

Starra was stern. She moved the tissue paper aside and looked in the bag. "Yes, he can but only one. He just started to eat solid food today and I don't want to cause stress in his digestive tract."

That brought a happy laugh out of Trey. "Wow. Homemade Christmas cookies? Really? I haven't had any since I was a kid. Let me see what you brought."

I handed him my gift bag. He was as cute as a little boy looking inside at the bag's contents like I had just handed him a bag of gold coins.

Nurse Andrews looked serious. "One, Trey. Only one."

Trey nodded. "Okay I understand but take a look at these. Jess made angels and Santas and reindeer. My Aunt Linda baked cookies like these for me every Christmas. You said you brought some to the Island Senior Center? You know that center was named after my great grandmother. The attendees must have loved these and you in your holiday outfit. Hmm. Tough choice but since I'm a carnivore, I think I'll eat a reindeer."

He took one out before Nurse Andrews confiscated the bag, placing it on his gift table that sadly had no other flowers, cards, or gifts. Trey munched his reindeer like Sam does his cookies. He laughed. "I feel better already. Thank you, Jess, for these cookies, your holiday spirit, and for taking care of Sam, I want to reimburse you for any expenses he caused. I know from your note that you took him to the vet, had him groomed and checked, and now have to feed him. He eats like a horse, you know."

I smiled. He seemed so nice like a regular guy, not all stuck up like a big shot lawyer. "Not a problem," I responded. "I'm glad I could help and you're right he loves his dog food and does eat like a horse. From what I've read about your accident, you're pretty lucky to be talking to us right now."

"I think I was very lucky. I'm lucky to be awake, very lucky to meet you, and lucky my Sam is all right. As I said, please tell me how expensive that little guy has been, and I'd be happy to reimburse you for his bills. Do you work?"

I hedged. "I'm an associate editor for an online travel magazine and contribute articles for publication, so I work from home. Sam loves that. Since he was lost, he wants to have me around him all the time."

Trey laughed. "I can't blame him for that. I always knew he was smart."

I continued. "Anyway, I took Sam to my former vet, Dr. Amy. I lost my own dog Mazy in October. Mazy was great and I miss her every day. From playing with Sam, I know you would have liked Mazy. Anyway, Dr. Amy told me she does pro bono work for a deserving animal each month and since we had to find out more about Sam's condition and his owner, she said he was her choice for this month."

Trey looked interested. "I appreciate what she did very much, but I can afford to pay her so she can work on another patient pro bono. When I get to the rehab facility, please bring me her address. I'd like to send her a donation so she can keep that good work of hers going."

Wow. He really is nice, but I hope his kindness isn't too good to be true. Does he think we'll remain acquaintances when he gets to rehab? I guess we will. After all, I do have Sam.

Trey's blue eyes looked directly into mine. "I hope you'll come back to visit me. These past few minutes, I've enjoyed your company more than you can imagine and would like to learn more about the beautiful lady who rescued my Sam."

I wondered if that comment was the remnant of his anesthesia speaking. I didn't tell him yet, but I hoped to come back tomorrow with Sam and stand below his window so he could see what great shape Sam was in. I didn't want to shock him so I should tell him now.

"Mr. Musgrove, I was thinking about bringing Sam here tomorrow. We would stand right below your window. Maybe one of the nurses would assist you to the window so you could look down at us. If I do bring Sam, I won't be able to come up to visit you in person, but I'll get your room extension from Nurse Andrews and we can talk on the phone, that way you can talk to Sam as well."

Nurse Andrews walked in on our conversation and interrupted. "Jess that's so sweet and thoughtful. Call me with the time of your arrival and we'll make it happen for Trey." She handed me a piece of paper. "Here's the direct number to this room."

Trey reached out for my hand. I placed my hand in his and he squeezed it. "Please call me Trey. That's very special of you to do that for me, but I can tell you're special." His eyes lingered in mine for a few minutes before adding, "Like I said, Sam is very fortunate to find a guardian angel like you while I am lucky to meet you, share in your kindness, and look into those beautiful big brown eyes."

My heart fluttered; my face flushed. I wondered if Trey could tell I was getting smitten. Just in time to save me from embarrassment, the lab tech entered the room. He was my excuse to leave. I waved on my way out the door. "See you tomorrow, Trey."

He shot me an irresistible smile. "I'm looking forward to it."

The tech pulled the curtain around Trey's bed as soon as I walked out of the room. Once in the hallway, I collapsed against the wall trying to catch my breath after meeting such a wonderful man. I had studied his photo before wondering if Trey would be as nice as he looked. Today, I found out he was even better.

The next day, I called Starra to let her know we'd be there by two today, before prepping Sam for our hospital visit. I brushed him, put on his jingle bell collar, and attached his leash. Placing my cell in my purse with a couple of his cookies, off we went. We arrived at Healthwell and I was lucky to find a parking space on the same side of the building as Trey's room. Sam and I walked the grounds as my eyes centered on those sixth-floor windows. Sweeping by the row of windows, I saw someone standing in the very center of the row, waving. By her white hair and white uniform, I could tell it was Starra. I dialed Trey's room and he surprised me by answering. Starra must have handed him the phone. "Hi, Jess.

I can't wait to see both of you. Give me a minute to get out of bed and go to the window."

Starra took charge. "Jess, please give us a few minutes to assist Trey to the chair by the window and call back."

I answered, "Of course." Sam and I walked around the area. He's still very puppyish and needs to exercise as much as possible.

After a few minutes, I looked up and saw two people waving from that same window so I called Trey's number again. Trey answered his voice sounding stronger today. "Hey, Jess. I'm feeling better, more like normal. The doc said my brain swelling has reduced quite a bit. Who's that with you? My best buddy?"

I put the phone on speaker so Sam could hear Trey's voice. "Sam, Sammy it's me Trey." I held the phone as close to Sam's ear as possible. After he heard Trey's voice, he started to jump around in circles. I forgot how strong Sam was. He put his paws on my shoulders licking my face before settling down to lick my cell. At this point, I didn't know if I could hold him until he heard Trey. "Be a good boy Sam. Don't jump. Sit."

Just like magic, Sam sat. He wouldn't do it that easily for me. I guess we know who the big dog in this group is. I told Trey, "Sam obeyed at once. I'm impressed with your dog training skills and so glad you're feeling better."

Starra interrupted us in the background. "The anesthesia usually wears off in a day or two. His took a little longer but he's fine now."

I was glad to hear that. "Sounds great to me. Trey, are you eating okay?"

"I am," he answered. "I lost my appetite yesterday probably from all the drugs, but I think your Christmas cookies turned the tide. I love the frosting on the Santas. Cherry?"

I laughed. "Yes, cherry. I'm glad they helped at least to

boost your spirits. I really wanted you to see Sam. He must have wandered around lost for a week with little or no food and more than likely drinking from puddles.

"When he came into my yard, besides being so filthy, I could see his rib cage. He looked tired and weak but look at him now. He eats dog food like a champ, plays with new squeaky toys, chews rawhide sticks, and just loves to boss me around. He hangs with me every second probably because after being lost for that week, he doesn't want to lose sight of me. The only time I leave him is to go to the grocery store, pharmacy or unless I come here of course. Even then, he's not alone. My retired neighbor stays with him. All of my friends love him, bring him treats and let me take him to their houses. He's been a good boy around my fresh Christmas tree and loves to put his head under the low hanging branches to nap under the lights. I don't want you to worry about him. He'll be with me until you can take him home."

Trey remained silent for a minute. "He's a very lucky dog. I wish I were that lucky. Thank you. That night, we were hit head on driving down the Beach Road, a two-lane road. It was dark and I hit my head so hard after my car crashed, I was unconscious when they brought me into the emergency room. Today, Dr. Jake paid me a visit and told me I kept calling out Sam's name until they administered the anesthesia. Jess, you have given me the best Christmas present ever, besides your cookies, that is. Trust me. I will make all this up to you."

I shook my head. "No need. There's nothing to make up. I love him and he's not a problem. I'm glad I could help you and keep this guy out of a shelter. Let me walk him around so you can see how great he's doing."

I took Sam's leash and walked him back and forth. He shook his head and since my call was still active, Trey could hear the jingle bells.

He came back on. "He looks amazing. And those jingle bells. Very festive."

We both laughed. Sam heard us and loved it, jingling them more. "My neighbor, Terry, brought them over the day after Sam arrived. I have to take them off at night otherwise I wouldn't get any sleep. I'm planning to visit you tomorrow. Would you like me to bring Sam?"

Trey responded, "Now that I've seen what great care Sam's received, I'd like to visit with you alone. As long as I keep on my current pace, tomorrow, being my fourth day out of the coma, may be my last day here before they move me into rehab."

"Where will they move you? Will it be far from here?" I asked.

Trey replied. "No. There's a facility associated with the hospital right across the street and set back from the road. Nurse Andrews suggested it because they let well behaved pets visit after a check of temperament from the front desk."

I was excited. "That sounds so great. We can come together. Sam will love that. I can tell by his reaction today he really misses you and loves you."

"And I love him," Trey responded before Nurse Andrews came on the line. "Jess, please come any time after two tomorrow. The doctors will be doing follow-up tests to make sure he can be transferred to rehab."

"I will and will call before I come. Trey, I'll see you tomorrow. Sam, say good-bye."

Like this smarty pants of a dog understood, Sam barked while I waved. When they were no longer standing in the window, we left for home wondering what our meeting today held in store for both of our futures.

CHAPTER 7

My editor-in chief e-mailed that my Lapland article was a go. She also said to check my post office box because she sent out end of the year checks. I forgot. How can I forget about getting money? Easy. One word. Sam.

I had most of the morning free before going to the hospital so I went to the island center to pick up my mail and visit our island grocery to buy more supplies for my Christmas Eve party. I know it was still two weeks away but stocking up on some of the baking supplies early helps. I can bake small loaf cakes and unfrosted cupcakes when I have time and freeze them.

My open house is an important tradition to me. I hope I can bring cheer to any lonely souls, as well as all of my friends and neighbors. I spent many holidays alone and wanted to help others in the same situation. My regular party goers contribute by bringing their favorite dish to share. We have an absolute feast and make new and wonderful friends.

I brought the mail and groceries home. Terry had already arrived and played fetch with Sam. For some reason, after putting on an island sundress, I felt like beautifying myself with make-up and hair gel. I finished and walked into the kitchen. Terry took one look at me. "Girl, you look like you're going on a date not to the hospital."

I wondered. "Is that bad?"

Terry chuckled. "No not at all. You look great. I think Mr. Musgrove's going to like it."

Arriving at the hospital a few minutes past two, I rushed to the elevator. As soon as the door opened, who should I see walking out but Jake. He smiled and let the door go preventing me from getting in. "You here again? You look extra nice today. That Trey Musgrove must really be something special."

I harrumphed. "I have his dog. Remember? I hope he gets better. I'm here for a very brief visit."

I waited for the next elevator and got off on the sixth floor. I went straight to ICU. No matter what Jake says or does, he still infuriates me. I took a deep breath to calm down from my Jake encounter before walking into Trey's room. When he saw me, his face lit up like a meteor as he studied me.

"Thanks for coming, Jess. You look beautiful." He paused. "I'll be moving over to rehab tomorrow and phoned Goldie, my housekeeper, to bring me enough clothes for seven days. I don't plan on staying there any longer than that. Will you and Sam visit me at rehab tomorrow at whatever time is good for you? I understand it may be hard with work and the holidays, but I hope you can make it. I'd love to see you."

My ears lingered on "Housekeeper." "You have a housekeeper?" I asked.

Trey laughed. "You are looking at Mr. Mess. I'm single, work long hours, and if I didn't have someone to take care of things and Sam when I'm not home, I'd tear my hair out and live like a caveman."

"Well, I'm Miss Mess, but I have to clean up after myself." I laughed.

That brought a smile to his face. "I guess we have a lot in common. How's my boy doing today?"

"Sam is excellent. Tonight he's in for a treat. Our island pet store has their annual Holiday Faire for pets and their owners. They give out samples of different food and treats and each pet has a lucky number for a prize drawing. I've been shopping there lately so that's how Sam and I got invited."

That brought a chuckle out of Trey. "This island of yours sure knows how to celebrate the holidays. This is Sam's first Christmas and I figured we'd be celebrating alone but since you came into our lives I have a feeling this year's going to be more than merry. Wish I were better and could go to the pet store with you."

"We wish you could too." I pondered.

Trey smiled. "Holiday traditions are very special. Why is it that the ones that got messed up are the ones we remember the most? You know my grandfather loved to put up a holiday light display on the magnificent flowering red bushes that surrounded his front porch. He reminded me every year of how special the white lights looked among the red flowers.

"Anyway, one year when I was ten, I went over to help him. He had us add so many lights to his display they shorted out and caused the bushes to catch fire. His neighbor called the fire department and they came right away and evacuated my grandmother and my visiting mother while putting the fire out. Funny, how that sticks in your memory. Do you have any tales like that?"

I put my hand over my mouth to hide a giggle. "I sure do. When I was five, I was asked to be the angel at the manger for our church's annual Christmas pageant. I put on my pink silky robe and had help attaching my fluffy wings but forgot to wipe the doughnut crumbs off my face. The cast had been treated to doughnuts before the play. When I came out with crumbs on my face and in my old sneakers because I forgot to put on the gold angel shoes, everyone in the pews I walked by laughed including my father who afterwards had to announce, 'My little angel was miscast as the Christmas angel.' That brought more laughter from the audience. Needless to say, I felt my dirty face and looked down at my shoes and blushed."

"You still are an angel, but I bet you were cute as heck back then too."

I glanced at my watch. "Oh, no, it's almost five. I'm going to have to run to feed and walk Sam before the pet party at six thirty. We should be back at home by nine. I can call you after we get home to let you know how Sam liked it. He is friendly with other dogs, isn't he?"

Trey flashed one of his irresistible smiles. "As long as they don't attack him first."

I placed my hand on my forehead to show stress. "This should be an interesting party to put it mildly. I'll call later. Talk to you then. Bye."

Trey waved as I walked out the door. "Thanks for everything. You've made this mess in my life fun."

I raced home to get Sam ready for the party and grab a quick bite for myself. Fed, watered, walked, and brushed, we left for Island Pets.

The Barking Dogs singing Jingle Bells blasted from Island Pets' outside speakers as we entered. All kinds of pets had already arrived. Dogs, birds in cages, fish in bowls and the ones I dreaded the most, cats. Only dogs and cats were eligible for the prize bags, but the others did get samples and I'm sure their owners loved to come and show them off. I was concerned because Mazy used to get in a tizzy fit every time she encountered a cat, but she was small. Sam outweighs any of these cats by a mile so he may have a different attitude.

Once inside, we greeted all the other pet owners who were

wonderful and so careful about keeping their animals and fish at a safe distance from any pets unfamiliar to them. Sam looked at all his new friends and puppy danced around my legs while still on his leash. Still young and naive, he noticed a big fluffy cat named Fruity and became very curious. He pulled me to Fruity who raised her back and hissed. Sam wagged his tail and was about to put his nose down to sniff her when I yanked him away. I didn't want Fruity to scratch him.

The party was so adorable, and I needed some holiday spirit after this past year so I was glad we came. There was an artificial tree set up with a cat angel on top. The lights were dog bones and the tinsel garlands fish shaped. The store employees wore green felt elf costumes and handed every pet owner a paper Santa bag in which to put our samples. Sam and I visited the different small tables.

Some elves gave out a treat to taste as well as a sample bag of product. By the time we finished, Sam had eaten at least ten small treats and had his Santa Bag full. Dan, the store owner, was dressed like Santa. He was perfect for the part being a little rotund in the tummy himself. He was in his sixties with pure white hair and a full white mustache. All he needed to add was the beard. By his cheerful demeanor, we all could see that Dan enjoyed the party as much as the pets.

His favorite part was taking photos with Santa. Any of his customers who wanted their precious companions, whether furry, feathery, or fishy alike, to pose with the jolly old guy himself had a chance to do so.

The elves took turns using a Polaroid and handed out the photo as soon as it printed. Sam was so happy he licked Santa's face and got a few strands of beard in his mouth. He tried as hard as he could to spit the strands out, but they were stuck. I had to help him. Everyone, including Dan, laughed. Dan called Sam back and gave him a big hug. Phone cameras as well as elves clicked like crazy because they were so sweet together. After the photos were finished, Dan passed around a tray of red and green mini cupcakes along with small cups of lemonade for the pet owners. I looked at my watch. Eight fifteen already? Why does time pass so quickly when you're having fun?

Dan walked to the front of the store to address this motley group of animal lovers. He began. "First, I want to thank you all for coming and for your loyal business all year long. Being a small local business, it means a great deal to me. Now we've come to the most exciting part of the evening, Our Annual Holiday Big Bag Drawing. As you can see there are three sizes of cat and dog gift bags on the counter next to me. All other pets will receive a five dollar gift certificate to thank you for your business. If you remember when you entered the store, one of our elves saw whether you brought a cat or dog and handed you a ticket with numbers on it. They immediately dropped the other half of the ticket in the appropriate bag for cat or dog."

Dan then held up a large blue bag with dogs printed on it. He shook it. "I'll draw for the smallest dog gift bag first working our way up to the very big one. Would elf Celine please come and mix up the tickets in my bag?"

Celine, a cute blonde high school student who worked part time after school, came to the front and mixed the tickets up with her hand. She handed the bag back to Dan who drew the first number. "Here goes, first ticket number is 33189276."

Silence until we all heard a scream, "That's us! Oh my gosh! We won! It's Sandy and Dudley." Sandy patted her black lab Dudley's head as she repeated. "Hey, Dudley, we won." Dudley barked, excited by the happy tone of his owner's voice.

Dan handed Sandy the bag as Dudley tried to get a whiff

of what inside smelled so good. Everyone raced to congratulate Sandy like contestants do at the end of the dog shows. Dan waved his hands in the air and continued to do so until he got everyone's attention. "Ready for ticket number two?" This time he picked a red bag with cats on it. Celine came back to shuffle the tickets. "This is for one lucky cat. Ticket number 33189290."

Another scream of joy as Sarah Moore and Fruity won that one. She held Fruity, a huge tabby, and bounced her up and down all the way to the front to receive her gift bag. Everyone congratulated Sarah but tried their best to keep the dogs away from the cats. We are all animal people so we're happy when anyone's animal thrives.

Dan cleared his throat. "I need a drumroll if we had one, that is. Now for the big dog bag. It's called that because it's loaded with dog stuff galore like treats, toys, shampoos, you name it it's in there. We've already mixed these tickets so here goes. Number 33189230."

I didn't look at our ticket. I felt no need since I never win but when no-one screamed, Dan asked. "Please look at your numbers once more. If no one claims this we'll have to draw again. Number 33189230."

Everyone looked at their tickets again this time including me. My hands shook so much with excitement. I almost dropped our ticket. "Oh, my gosh," I exclaimed. "It's us."

Sam danced around on his leash as we went to collect our prize because he could tell I was happy. He knew by my voice it had to be something wonderful. I accepted our bag. Teary eyed, I hugged Dan to thank him.

"Thank you. My goodness I'm still surprised. I didn't look at my ticket the first time because I've never been lucky and never won anything in my life. Sam is now going to have the best first Christmas ever."

Dan hugged me back and petted Sam as the other pet

parents applauded our win. Most of them knew about his situation.

"Congratulations!" we heard from every direction. I just couldn't believe we won. "Thank you all so much, especially Dan and his elves for this wonderful party."

Sam adored all the attention. The black and white cat clock with a moving tail on the store's front wall read eight thirty. We didn't want to overstay our welcome so we thanked everyone again and headed for the front door. Odd, I thought I heard wind chimes, but we were inside. The sounds followed us so we turned around to see our island's self-proclaimed psychic Emerald Moon. She wore her usual multi-colored and multi layered gauze skirt in gold, red, avocado green, and royal blue with a gypsy style white blouse. Emerald attended the party to announce she had just adopted a kitten she named Charm from the shelter. Her arms were the wind chimes jingling at least a dozen silver bangles. She grabbed onto my arm and stopped me short as I opened the front door.

"I overheard your comment about your past luck and can sense your pain after losing Mazy. I feel the depth of your sorrow. I lost my own ten-year-old cat this past year as well. Even though I communicate with her spirit every day, I still do miss her terribly."

Emerald Moon, her jet-black hair with a sprinkle of white showing at her temples, had her hair tied back with a turquoise silk scarf. As she looked deep into my eyes with her green ones, I felt shivers race up my spine. Her stare alone gave me the creeps, never mind that she had placed her right hand with a silver ring on each finger to touch my Sam's forehead. Emerald gently closed his eyes and keeping her hand over his gazed up at the ceiling. Everyone nearby became silent; they knew better than to upset her. She was eccentric even if you didn't believe in her hokey pokey. Her eyes turned to Sam as she started to speak.

"You all know I've been doing psychic readings of animals as well as people on this island for the past fifteen years ever since I completed my spiritual training. I allowed my psychic senses to release their powers into Sam's mind. Right now, I know through my communal vibrations with your dog, that he was sent to change your life, your love life, and your luck forever."

Okay, that all sounded good, but I wondered how Sam was holding up. Sam didn't mind her hand over his eyes. After all, it was attention and for some reason he liked sniffing it, maybe because she had been holding Charm. She removed her hand from his eyes and waved both her hands in front of my face in a swirling motion I guess to solidify her prophesy of future good luck. Since I didn't know how Sam would take all the swirling, I held onto Sam's leash tighter as well as his giant Big Dog bag full of treats and toys. As soon as she finished, I thanked her and left hearing the chatter of the other attendees continue inside.

What an out of this world evening! Wait until I tell Trey.

The more I told Trey about our evening, especially the part about Emerald Moon, the harder he laughed. All he could say was, "I wished I could have been there just to see the looks on both of your faces after you won and later reacting to that psychic. Sam must have gone crazy. The more I think about that animal psychic, the funnier your story gets."

"Sam did go crazy after we won. You know, if you're out of the hospital by Christmas, I'll send that giant Santa bag home with you so Sam can celebrate in style."

Trey paused, "I have a strong feeling we'll all be celebrating together, and I'll make sure all of us have a wonderful Christmas."

I thought that was an odd thing to say since we've only

known each other a brief time and more than likely won't be together after he goes home.

Trey changed the subject. "My first day in rehab tomorrow is totally filled up. I had hoped you two would visit me tomorrow, but they've scheduled a gazillion tests and frown on any visitors until my second day. I hope I will see you and Sam then. Sam has to get approved at the visitor desk before you both can come to my room. I have a physical therapy session early that morning and a doctor's check at noon. If you can come later that afternoon, I would be so happy to see you both."

Listening to his sexy voice, how could I say "no"? "Can I bring you anything special when we come?"

Trey paused, then he said, "I can't think of anything better than you and Sam. Goodnight, Jess and thank you for being so wonderful to Sam and me."

"Good night, Trey. Good luck tomorrow. We'll talk again tomorrow evening."

I hung up and wondered if I was in for a huge let down once Trey recuperated. He will leave me and so will Sam. But I am getting involved with my eyes wide open and well aware of the pitfalls. For now, I'll put my doubts aside and enjoy my time in the present with them. I looked at Sam. He was already asleep on his quilt. Overhearing Trey's voice on my phone tonight made him relax after enjoying the exciting evening we both shared. After all, we won and hope our winning streak will continue in more ways than one.

Today, Sam woke up brighter eyed and bushier tailed than usual, excited to get his day started. He jumped up to wake me with wet doggy kisses. I knew that was dog talk for "I need my walk" so I threw on my jean shorts and a shirt and took him outside. After which, we both had a hearty breakfast.

Morning coffee woke my brain causing me to panic realizing I had only eight days left until my Christmas Eve party.

Since my open house was a yearly thing, no formal invites were necessary, but I liked doing them anyway because they made my guests feel special. I especially appreciate our island shrimpers attending. Not only are they fun and colorful to talk to, but they love to help and bring big plastic bags of shrimp packed in ice. They like to drop the bags off earlier that afternoon so I can prepare mounds of shrimp cocktail. I mix my own cocktail sauce and thank them with every bite.

Breakfast and Sam duties finished I went to my computer to send out a few more invites by e-mail. I sent them to as many houses, businesses, and shrimp boats as I had addresses. What fun! Crazy I know, but I've never had a problem with anyone attending and always felt safe. Besides, I knew those shrimpers would take care of anyone giving me a hard time.

As soon as I sat down at my desk, there was a knock on my front door. Sam barked so I went to peek through the semi-sheer window curtain on my door. Surprised to say the least, I saw Jake standing there. Jake? What does he want now? He only comes when he needs something except now to bring dog food for Sam. I spoke to him curtly through the door. "What do you want now?"

He shot me one of his phony smiles through the curtain. "Ah shucks, Jess, is that any way to greet the man you almost married? I just want to talk and ask for your advice."

Hmmm. Not like him at all to take advice from me but being curious, the holidays, and worst of all my being a soft touch, I told Sam to step aside and against my better judgement opened the door.

"Come in. Would you like some coffee?"

Jake grinned. "Jess, you're the best. I sure would."

He followed me and Sam into the kitchen and sat down at my kitchen table like old times as I put on my coffee pot. By his frown lines and the uncomfortable way he squirmed on his seat, he looked like he had something important on his mind and it wasn't going to be something I liked.

"Well," he began. "I've got some good news and some bad news." Right there I knew he was up to something. He continued. "The good news is I want to marry Barbie. The bad news is I can't propose yet because I can't find my grandmother's ring."

CHAPTER 8

B ingo. There it is. The real reason for his visit. I kept
that ring after he broke up with me, after he cheated on
me, and since at the time, he never asked for it back. I
decided I deserved that ring for putting up with all his
nonsense.

Jake continued. "Mom wanted me to give her mother's
ring to the woman I was going to marry. By the way, Jess, we
both would want you to come to the wedding."

If he hoped that comment would make me feel any better
about giving back the ring, it didn't, but I held back my anger
to let him continue and see where he was going with this.

"Anyway, since our break-up, I can't find it. Do you know
what I might have done with it?"

That snake knew exactly what happened to it. By his
refusal to ask for it back, he knew his silence allowed me to
keep it. Coffee ready, I poured us two cups and got the pitcher
of cream from my fridge. Since I didn't respond to his
question right away, he kept going. "I seem to remember you
were the last one to wear it."

Last one? I asked myself. Were there more? He became
concerned when I didn't respond. "Jess, let's not have hard

feelings about this. I wanted us to move forward on good terms. You didn't sell or pawn it, did you?"

Silent, I listened slowly sipping my coffee and shook my head "no" as he continued.

"That diamond ring symbolized our love for each other at that point in time, but now that's no longer the case."

Symbolize. That's a big word for a former surfer and high school football player. How insensitive can this man be? How can he just put aside the love we had for each other with "that's no longer the case?" Ugh. Just the thought of Barbie getting my gorgeous engagement ring made my stomach churn.

What to do? Since I possessed the ring, I knew I was in charge of this situation. I became so incensed by his lack of feelings that I had to get up from the table and leave him alone to control my emotions so I could decide what to do. "Excuse me for a few minutes, Jake. I have to think about this."

I stood and went back into my bedroom. Sam followed me all the way. I opened my dresser drawer, took out my jewelry box, and lifted its lid. The first thing that caught my eye was my Granny Meta's ruby and diamond ring. My grandfather gave it to her for their fiftieth wedding anniversary. Imagine sharing fifty years of love while my engagement to Jake didn't even last one year.

The antique gold setting was shaped like a flower with small rubies filling each of the five petals, one to denote each decade of love. Set in its center was a small round brilliant diamond. Granny always told me she wanted me to wear her ring on my right hand on my wedding day. To make sure I would, she left it to me in her will. "Something old" she used to remind me.

I always treasured Granny Meta's advice. I wished she was here with me now. My mind drifted back to the school year I didn't make cheerleading squad. I was crushed and disappointed. When I told her about it, she said, "Jessica, remember, sometimes, even when it doesn't seem so, bad things can happen for the best." She was right because soon after that, I was selected to be an exchange student to study art history in Florence, Italy. I lived with a wonderful family and had access to the most famous museums in the world and would have had to give up cheerleading in order to go. Maybe she's watching over me now trying to send me that same advice. I sat back thinking how Jake's breaking up with me, no matter how hard it was, may have been for the best, my best. How could any woman in her right mind live with a two-timing man like him and not worry that it wouldn't happen again. I took a deep breath realizing how glad I'll be to get that man out of my life and heart for good.

With that thought in mind, I took out the velvet box that contained my former engagement ring. I opened it, held the ring in my hand and tried it on all the while admiring how beautiful it was, and remembering how much it had meant to me about our future together, and my love for a man with whom I wanted to spend the rest of my life. I then realized it was just a piece of jewelry, one that no longer meant any of those things to me since that dream of a man became my worst nightmare for heartbreak and pain.

Now that same ring reminded me of how he broke my heart, how he destroyed my dreams, and how his leaving me for another woman caused me to spiral into depression especially after losing Mazy. Thank goodness, I am no longer sad about our break-up but remain angry at how he disrespected me.

I was just keeping that ring out of spite so he couldn't give it to anyone else, especially Barbie. I should walk out there and tell him I suddenly remembered that I did sell it, but instead took the ring into the kitchen. I really wanted to throw it in his face but instead shoved the box in front of him on the table. What's the old saying, "There's nothing worse than a woman scorned." I looked Jake straight in the eyes. "Here's your ring. Give it to Barbie. She may have better luck wearing it than I did. I no longer need it or want it, especially since I'd like to remove any trace of you from my heart."

Jake looked puzzled. "Was I that bad to you?"

"What kind of stupid question is that? Yes, you sure were. You shattered my heart into a million little pieces. I'm just now getting through it. So take your stupid ring and go make Barbie happy."

That tough guy had tears in his eyes. "Jess, I really did care for you and still do just in another way. You know I'd help you any way I could. I hope someday you'll forgive me and let me back into your life. I didn't mean to fall in love with Barbie. It just happened."

I'm sure he wasn't here to explain. His only desire was to get the ring back. Sam came by. That furry angel could tell I was stressed and licked my knee.

"Just happened, huh? Well, here's what's happening now. I no longer want to see you, talk to you unless medically necessary about Trey, and want you out of my life. You know where the door is. Use it."

He stood and leaned over to kiss the top of my head but I turned away so he couldn't. Ring box in hand, he left saying, "Thank you, Jess. You truly are a Christmas angel." Since he got what he came for, he opened the door and left.

Seems like I've been a guardian angel quite a bit lately, maybe I need one myself. I sat in the kitchen and placed my head down on the table with Sam by my side remembering my Granny's words. "Sometimes things happen for the best."

I tried as hard as I could not to let Jake's visit spoil my day. I finished my invites and wondered how Trey's first day in rehab went. Better yet, I thought about spending the afternoon with him tomorrow. A knock on my front door interrupted my thoughts. I peeked out my front door window hoping Jake didn't return when I saw Terry unloading two large cardboard boxes from his trunk.

I watched him carry each one separately onto my front porch unaware that I saw him. He knocked again only to see my smiling face staring back at him through the window.

He laughed. "While some of us sleep late, others of us are up at an early hour ready to battle the ever-exhausting yard sales. Now, Sleeping Beauty, please let me come in."

I made him wait a few minutes before opening the door. "You know Terry I wasn't sleeping. I was busy sending out more open house invites."

Terry shot me a superior look. "Well, that's great considering I went to this absolutely fabulous moving sale with Rich to help decorate for your party." He shoved the door open to push his way by me and leave the first box on my front hall table before going back outside for the second.

I took a quick look inside. There had to be a hundred things in those two boxes all having to do with Christmas. Terry caught his breath. "Whew I'm not the young stud I used to be. Most of this stuff is for your party." He clapped his hands. "Rich and I will take home anything that's left."

I shrugged. "Please take them home now. I already have enough on my plate."

Terry smiled. "When you didn't call this morning to watch Sam, I assumed you weren't going to the hospital to see Trey. At that point, I thought this sale might be a moving experience. Get it?"

I chuckled and made a face at his bad joke. "Got it. So what are you going to do with this stuff?"

Terry grinned like a Cheshire cat. "Not I, we. If you dig a little deeper in each box you will find brand new outdoor holiday LED lights. Seeing how you've had a bad year in more ways than one, we are going to turn your cottage into a virtual winter wonderland. It will be so beautiful it will make anyone passing by feel like a kid again. Besides some extra cheer and love helps heal a broken heart."

I still wasn't interested. "I have no time for such nonsense. As you can see, I already decorated."

Terry pointed to the boxes again. "Ah yes, but not for the Beach Holiday Light Festival. These boxes contain at least a million outdoor lights along other fun decorations. Most are all still in their original unopened boxes and all meet the current codes. Oh, another wonderful Terry pun! They just keep coming. Anyway, I don't think the couple who bought this stuff planned on moving before they used the decorations. The wife was very personable and told me at the sale that her husband who worked for a bank received a big promotion at a branch out of state. I felt funny buying all this at such a cheap price, but she said they couldn't take everything with them."

I rifled through the boxes. He was right. They contained all brand new stuff. "Maybe they got caught shoplifting." I chuckled.

"Very funny. You know the Beach newspaper has a contest each year for the most lit-up house on the island. They give a one hundred fifty dollar Island Steakhouse gift certificate to the winner. That means when your house wins because of my hard work, the three of us can go to the Island Steak House for a fancy lunch. Now, Miss Smarty Pants, what do you think of that?"

"When my house wins? Funny, I don't remember entering."

Terry paused. "Actually you didn't. Rich and I entered your house after we bought all these amazing decorations because we wanted to help you with that wonderful open house you host every year. We wanted to make it extra special for you and your guests. Besides, we enter ours every year and even won last year."

"More decorations for my open house actually sounds

pretty good to me now." I wondered. "It's one o'clock now. How long will it take us to hang all these lights?"

"With two of us working, I'd say we'd be done by five. So let's get busy. The contest judges ride by tomorrow evening after five thirty and that steak sounds so good I'm already getting hungry."

We moved both boxes to my kitchen floor and started to empty the contents spreading them out to see what exactly we had. I held up one of the many small boxes. "Hey, Terry, did you know most of the decorations are pink, my favorite color. Look at these pink flamingo lights," I gushed. "I love them."

He laughed. "Now that's the spirit. They will accent your pink and silver theme. They say somewhere in the world there's a duplicate for everyone. Maybe we found your sister in pink at the sale."

I didn't even know I had a theme, but I allowed Terry to be in charge. We dangled the flamingo lights from my porch roof, added silver sparkling lights to the bushes in front of my house. There were even pink and white plastic candy canes to line my walk, and a giant inflatable snowman. Wow! Where did these people find all of this?

"Okay," Terry added, "now for the super long extension cords I found in box number two." He pulled the long cords out like a snake charmer, removed the tags, and attached them to the lights in the order we hung them. He then reached into his pocket and pulled out three light timers for our display. "Now that I have all of the display connected with the extension cords and can see you have outlets on the porch so all we need to do is set these timers. What time would you like your winter wonderland with all of its magic to start?"

I answered still amazed by his organization. "You thought of everything. How about setting the opening time for five thirty, that's right around dusk and off at ten thirty?"

Terry responded, "That should be long enough to make the power company happy."

He tried to calm my fear of a huge electric bill. "These are new and LED lights that use very little electricity and give off little or no heat."

I wiped my forehead. "Whew! That's a relief. I can't wait to see them lit now."

My neighbor went to work setting the timers. When he was done, I invited him inside for iced tea while we waited for the lights to come on. I laughed, "Terry, you sure can make a boring day fun."

"Oh, my dear there's more to this day than you know. My personal chef Rich is making homemade marinara sauce, meatballs and spaghetti along with garlic bread, salad, and brownies. He's bringing our dinner over for us at five forty-five to celebrate our lighting event. He can't wait to see the lights either. After all, he did come with me to the moving sale and helped negotiate. We are going to have a feast."

I exclaimed, "All my fav foods, I can't wait. Since we only have a short time before our light show comes on, I'd better take Sam for a walk so he can enjoy his dog food while we feast."

Sam and I went outside. We returned just five minutes before all the lights came on. We sat on the porch with Terry and watched in awe. I felt like I was in a winter wonderland especially watching the falling snowflake lights. Sam watched all the lights with his tail straight up. He probably had never seen anything like this in his short life. It was just beautiful.

I touched Sam's head thinking how lucky I was to have him if even for a short time, to have Terry and Rich in my life, and to have met Trey. I was glad he improved enough to transfer into rehab.

Rich came outside to break my thoughts and waved us inside. "Hurry up, you three. No one likes cold pasta and meatballs, especially me."

We hurried inside to find the table set, the wine poured, candles lit, and the salad and pasta placed in the center. Sam's nose went up sniffing the air in the direction of the meatballs. Rich had even filled Sam's dish with food before we came in.

I sat down feeling like a princess with all this service. We ate and laughed and drank wine until we finished the bottle. "I can't thank you both enough for this; the lights, the dinner, and most of all the fun. I haven't felt this great about my life and the holidays in months. As of tonight, I'm officially ready to celebrate Christmas."

Rich responded, "And so are we. Your open house will be the best one ever. Now comes the best part of dinner, my homemade brownies."

Rich got up, opened a plastic container, and arranged the deep dark chocolate treats on holiday plates he brought from home. I suddenly remembered, "I have French Vanilla ice cream in the freezer. Any takers?"

Everyone raised their hands. So vanilla ice cream it was. I gave Sam a cup of doggie ice cream I just bought, and he loved it. Sam was really well behaved tonight. I know he likes the boys and sensed how happy they made me.

After we finished our delicious dessert, Terry said, "Let's go back outside and admire our lights one more time. Those judges would be crazy to choose another house. Dishes can wait."

I clicked Sam to his leash, and we walked to the sidewalk next to the street to admire our lights. They remained a gorgeous winter wonderland. "I feel like a kid again," I gushed. Neighbors walking past my cottage loved the colors and twinkling lights.

We went back inside to clean up and I glanced at my cell. "Poor Trey. He left five messages asking where I was and if I was all right."

Terry laughed. "I think that guy really likes you. We got this, go ahead and call him back."

I left my two elves to clean the kitchen and went into my living room. Sam followed so close his paws touched my heels. I called Trey's new number in rehab that he left on my cell.

He answered, "Jess, I'm so relieved you called. I was worried when you didn't answer my calls. Are you and Sam all right?"

Surprised by his concern, I laughed. "Yes we both are fine. I haven't had anyone worry about me like this in years. It's kind of nice because my ex never did. I became lost in a project with Terry. It was long, tedious, and I didn't keep track of time."

Trey was curious. "Sounds interesting. What kind of project was it?"

"Well," I began, "Terry along with his partner Rich, went to a moving sale and bought two huge boxes of holiday lights and decorations. He thought we could light up my yard just in time for the Beach Holiday Light Festival. The judging begins tomorrow evening at five thirty. The anonymous contest judges drive up and down all the island streets in search of the best decorated house using holiday lights. My pink cottage looks so pretty. The decorations they purchased were all in pink, white, and silver. We put up thousands of lights on the front porch and along the bushes. I think aliens will be able to see my house from outer space. I doubt if we'll win, but we made an amazing entrance to my party."

Trey laughed. "Remember what I told you about my grandfather's Christmas lights."

I answered, "You know I actually thought about that as we were decorating. The lights Terry bought are brand new in the box LED lights. He said he went to the sale because he didn't have to watch Sam this morning. He's an early bird so yard and moving sales are his specialty. I know what you're thinking, it's eight o'clock now. How long did this take? We finished a little before five thirty and Rich brought over homemade spaghetti and meatballs, garlic bread and salad and the most delicious chocolate brownies I ever tasted for dessert. I added vanilla ice cream."

Terry added, "Wow. That sure beats this rehab food any day. May I come over for dinner once I'm out of here?"

"You are welcome anytime and so is Sam."

Trey added, "Beach people sure know how to party. Pet parties, senior center parties, boat parade, bar-b-ques. You make my city life sound boring."

"How could that be? You're an in demand divorce attorney and live downtown in very trendy surroundings?"

"City living is so different from the Beach's casual lifestyle. We dress in suits for functions, meet people at fancy socials, and seem to be always about promoting ourselves. I'm sure some older residents aren't like that but my age group sure is. Right now it sounds good to be able to kick back and enjoy myself. The more you tell me about your life, the more I might consider moving to the island."

I paused. "You'd be welcomed by everyone I know, but the downside is that you'd have a long commute to work in tourist season. Our infamous island traffic." I reminded him.

"I guess," he said reluctantly. "Are you still planning on coming to see me with Sam tomorrow? I miss you both so much when you're not here."

That was nice to hear, but I still had to remind myself not to let go of my heart too soon.

"We'll be there with bells on literally with Sam's jingle bells."

Trey laughed. "You make all this misery fun for me. Thank you. I'm looking forward to seeing you both."

I could hear Terry's voice coming from my kitchen, "Jess we're done and leaving. See you tomorrow."

I covered my phone, "Thank you both for everything. Love you."

I apologized for our interruption. "I called out to Rich and Terry who just finished the spaghetti clean-up and were heading home. I'm looking forward to seeing you tomorrow as well. Anything I can bring?"

"No. Just come. As I said before, you and Sam are all I need."

We hung up. I took Sam out for his evening walk mesmerized by my lights and Trey's attention.

With increased holiday traffic, I knew in order to reach the rehab center near Healthwell by three that afternoon I had to leave by two. Since I woke up early and thought I had little to do, two o'clock would be a piece of cake. Or would it? A knock on my front door was about to interrupt my newly acquired piece of mind.

Knock. Knock. Knock. Sam got wind of this way before I did and ran to the front door barking. I opened the door a crack to see a delivery guy in uniform holding a gigantic cardboard box. "Ms. Jessica Munroe?"

Since he wasn't from the pound or the sheriff's department, I nodded. He put the box down and handed me his clipboard. "Please sign here, ma'am."

I took his clipboard and signed my name. He tipped his hat which I thought was old fashioned but cute before going on his way. Now how on earth am I going to get this thing in the house?

I heard a car in my driveway. Oh great! More company to disturb my peaceful morning. I felt my blood pressure rise when I recognized Jake's black jaguar. Not him again, but at least this time he'll be good for something since, if nothing else, he was physically strong. Jake got out of his car whistling. He saw me on the porch and waved as happy as a clam.

"Great news!" he yelled out to me. "She said, 'yes.'"

Why on earth he thought I'd be happy about that, I don't know. He bounced onto the porch, threw his arms around me, and lifted me to give me a big bear hug. I fought like a bear, pounding on his shoulders for him to put me back down.

"Easy Jess, you know I wouldn't hurt you." He put me down "You are the best...the very best. I gave Barbie the engagement ring. Please may I come in and tell you all about it?"

I was surprised he thought I'd enjoy hearing about this but at the very least this was my big chance to get help with that enormous package.

"Jake, this package just arrived, and I wondered if you'd help me drag it inside."

Jake looked at the package. "Wow, that is one big box. Supplies for the party? That's one of the other things I wanted to talk to you about."

I shook my head "no" to party supplies as he picked up this enormous box and carried it inside to my front hallway.

"Thank you for helping with that."

I thought at the very least, he's strong enough to move that box if nothing else. He placed the box down in my hall and started to head for my kitchen, but I held my hand up like a school crossing guard to stop him from entering my house any further than the front hall. "Jake, I thought I made this clear. I want nothing more to do with you and couldn't care less about hearing about your proposal to Barbie. Why you want to open those sore wounds that broke my heart, I can't imagine. Please leave."

He looked at me like a deer in the headlights. "But Jess, we've known each other since junior high school. Remember all those good times we had together."

His last statement made me remember how and when Jake and I fell in love. We're both islanders, born and bred. We attended the same junior high and went on to high school together. Back then, we were never attracted to each other. I dated geeks; he cheerleaders. It was not until he came back to the area to complete his internship that sparks began to fly between us. We fell in love and got engaged until that is he met Barbie. When he broke up with me, he broke my heart. I was devastated especially since it happened so close to when I lost my Mazy. Crushed by both events, Trey and Sam now bring new feelings of caring and hope that make it easier to rid Jake from my life.

I was firm. I wanted to be as I answered him.

"I do remember but like you said before, 'had'. Had is the operative word here. Those days are as over as we are."

I walked around him and opened my front door. He shrugged his shoulders and left. Sam watched all of this and after Jake left came over to nudge my knee. That little guy made me realize even more how lucky I am to have Trey and Sam in my life for whatever time we all share together. I was determined not to let that snake of a former fiancé ruin my chance at true love.

CHAPTER 9

Once I heard Dr. Evil's car drive away, I left Sam sniffing every inch of that big box and went to get a pair of scissors from my desk drawer to open our mystery package. The label was addressed to Sam and me, but the package was from a fancy gourmet market downtown and not on the island. Sam sat next to me while I sliced through the packing tape. He sniffed the air. There must be something real good in there for him. I opened the box to find a holiday greeting card on the top of the package's contents. It read.

"To my Jess and Sam, enjoy this with my complements. Love, Trey."

I took the card out and removed the packing papers to see what was inside. It was loaded with all kinds of holiday treats. Christmas biscuits for Sam shaped like bells. He saw me take that box out and came over to try and paw it open. There were more surprises inside including a beautiful large white wicker gift basket filled with all kinds of fancy chocolates and chocolate dipped cookies. In its center was a large ornament, an angel all dressed in pink with silver wings. She had dark brown hair like mine and was beautiful. I took the basket out of the box and noticed another note attached to its wrapping.

"Thank you for being my Christmas angel. You make my holiday and Sam's magic. Love, Trey."

"Love Trey." Those two words sounded so wonderful to me. I looked under the basket to find two more boxes of holiday treats for Sam, one peanut butter and the other sweet potato cookies. Sam wagged his tail like crazy. He knew they were his. Trey didn't have to do this, but his surprise was so thoughtful and wonderful. I placed the basket in the center of my dining room table. It was so pretty I hated to open it. I looked closer at the angel. She had brown eyes like mine. How sweet! I loved chocolate and there was so much there I could eat some and save some for the party. My cell rang interrupting our drooling.

Trey asked, "Hi. Sweetie, did you get my package?"

"I did." I sighed. "It's so lovely. I've never received anything like it before."

Trey laughed. "Good. I'm happy I could do something nice for you both. Still coming at three? I'm on a lunch break right now so I could sneak this call."

I laughed. "How could I not come after you sent me all this chocolate? We'll see you at three. I'd better hurry, it's already one thirty."

We hung up. I changed into a skirt and blouse, fixed my make-up, and took Sam for his walk. Just as we were about to get into my car, I saw Terry running over, "Hey you. Remember the holiday light police are judging tonight at dusk. Rich and I will come over at five. Since I already have a key, I'll make sure everything is on and works."

I waved, saying, "Thanks. You're the best. I'll bring the three of us Mexican tonight from Eddy's Tacos." Terry looked happy. "That's one of our favorites."

I gave Sam a boost into my backseat and we left for the rehab center.

A young man wearing a name badge "Skip" greeted us at the front door of the rehab center. He escorted us to his desk where he asked for my ID and the name of the patient we were visiting. Then his glance turned to Sam. Of course I knew beforehand that Sam would have to stop at the front desk to get his temperament tested and show proof he had received all of his shots.

I had a print out with me from the vet of current vaccination records found in Sam's bone charm. Happy with the information, Skip then advised that he had to be sure of Sam's temperament. Since Sam was quite a large dog, Skip gave him the once over first. "Most of our visiting dogs are not this large. Does he bite?"

I couldn't help myself, "Only if you bite first." I laughed. He looked at me, puzzled, probably wondering if my response was a joke.

Skip took a deep breath. "Okay let's do this," he said. "Please hold him around the neck so I can see how he reacts to me when I touch him."

I was about to ask about his next of kin but decided he might not take that comment as a joke either. Skip let Sam sniff his hand first. Sam sat up straight as an arrow and let the young man pet him. "He likes this," Skip exclaimed surprised.

I answered. "Sam loves any and all attention. Did he pass the exam?"

Sam sniffed again before licking Skip's hand. The attendant leaned down only to get his face licked. "He's fine, fun actually. Anytime you want to talk to Mr. Musgrove alone, Sam's welcome to stay here with me. Before I get distracted, Mr. M's room is four-twenty-six, but you are a little early. I've been asked to have you wait fifteen minutes while the nurses get him ready for your visit. If you'd like, take Sam for a walk around the front of the building."

I could if Skip would stop petting him. He added, "He's one great dog. He passed with flying colors."

Skip finally removed his hand from Sam's back. I thanked him and took out Sam's holiday collar before confirming

Trey's room number. "You said room number four-twenty-six down the hall to the right."

Skip nodded the affirmative. I put the jingle bells on Sam, and we went outside for fifteen minutes. Patients out there for an assisted walk as well as those in wheelchairs just adored him. Sam spent most of his time getting petted. I looked at my watch. Time up, we went to see Trey. He heard Sam's collar jingle before we entered.

"Who's there?" he asked. "Is that Santa? I'm going to take a wild guess and say that's my Sam and Jess? Hurry, I can't wait to see you."

When Trey saw the two of us together his face lit up like the Statue of Liberty's torch. I chuckled. "Skip gave us quite the thorough security check. I think Sam made him nervous at first because of his size but now he and Skip are best buds."

Trey looked at Sam lovingly. "And why am I not surprised by that? How about a hug from my big guy?"

I let Sam loose and he went bounding over to greet Trey putting his front paws on Trey's lap to give him wet doggie kisses. Trey was happy to hold his dog. Dressed in gray running shorts and a solid yellow T-shirt, he sat in a big comfy recliner near the window. An attendant, who was in the hall at the time Sam and I entered Trey's room, brought a straight back chair in for me to use. I thanked her and sat next to Trey. She closed the door part way and left.

"Trey, you look great and seem so relaxed. Would you like to know more about the Beach Holiday Light Festival that Terry and Rich tricked me into? The judging is tonight. Secret judges selected by our Town Council will drive up and down our streets between five thirty and seven to evaluate all the addresses entered. I guess they have to remain secret so as not to receive any bribes, like homemade fudge."

Trey looked curious. "That's fast. Didn't you just enter yesterday?"

"No I didn't, but my two sneaky neighbors entered my

house online from Rich's cell right after they purchased those amazing decorations."

Trey planted a kiss on Sam's head as Sam got back down on the floor. "They do like to have fun with you. I think that's great. So tell me, do you have to be home by five thirty?"

"No. Since Terry and Rich decided to buy the lights from a moving sale, help me decorate, and enter my house in the contest without my knowledge, they will set everything up and wait for the judges. They said they did all of this to make my Christmas Eve open house extra special this year. The guests are going to love it. Besides, Rich added during dinner that pink wouldn't go with their traditional decorations and since they already won last year, they didn't want the judges to think they were greedy. I was so surprised by this especially since they usually enter their own house. I can't help but love those two guys. They make life fun. So my only task is to stop by Eddie's Tacos and bring home some tacos and Mexican food."

"The more you tell me about your life, the more I like this island lifestyle. I didn't know you were a fan of Mexican food," he replied.

"I'm not, but they are big time. I thought since they did most of the work on this project, they deserve to be treated even though my stomach doesn't fare well with all the spice," I replied. "Don't worry, I'll watch Sam like a hawk to make sure he doesn't pick up any scraps from the floor. We don't need another trip to the vet."

I opened my big purse. For some reason Sam sniffed around the top, I'm sure thinking everything inside was for him. He was almost correct. Before I could remove anything, the same attendant who brought in my chair, surprised us with a plate of chocolate cupcakes decorated with red and green sprinkles. She placed them on the dresser and left. Trey smiled.

"I thought you might like these knowing how much you

love chocolate. The kitchen advised us at breakfast that we could order cupcakes today for all our visitors. So I did since you are my one and only guest, besides Sam that is."

"And they even have chocolate frosting. That's so sweet, but I might wait to have one until a little later." My hand dove back into my bag again and I pulled out a package of four wrapped truffles from my gift basket and of course a large bone biscuit for Sam whose tail went ballistic at the sight of it. I gave Sam his cookie and held up my truffles.

"Would you like to try one of these? They were in that amazing basket you sent me." I jiggled the small package in the air. Trey replied, "That basket was for you."

"I know but I like to share," I answered tearing off the plastic wrap from the package. I got up and walked over to put one in Trey's hand before placing one in mine. "Let's have a contest. On the count of three, the first one to put a truffle in his or her mouth wins. Ready?"

He laughed. "That's a contest I can easily win. Ready? One. Two. Three." We raced to get the gold foil wrappers off. I was quicker and popped that delicious morsel in my mouth to melt and get the full flavor of the chocolate. "I won." I lifted my hands in the air making a victory symbol as we both chuckled.

"Come over here closer you little cheater," he said.

CHAPTER 10

"Cheater, huh?" I answered as he grabbed me by the shoulders and pulled me forward for a long lingering kiss. When our lips parted, he looked into my eyes, "I've been waiting to do that ever since the first moment I met you."

I was stunned and had to admit I enjoyed that kiss more than the chocolate. Evidently so did Sam because his tail wagged so hard, the breeze from his tail wagging cooled down our hot romantic moment.

Trey winked. "Got another one of those darn soft chocolates? Race you again?"

I went back to my purse to get the other two.

"You, my man, are on. I'll win again for sure." I handed him one and kept the other in my hand. "Ready on the count of three. One Two…"

Before I could say "Three", he pulled me again this time so I fell on to his lap. In the meantime, using one hand, Trey removed the wrapper and popped the chocolate into his mouth before I could open my hand to unwrap mine. He kissed me again. I didn't stop him. I wrapped my arms around his neck and caressed him as he deepened the kiss. Not wanting that delicious kiss to end, I sat on his strong lap enjoying his undivided attention for so long we lost track of time.

A nurse in uniform with a name tag that read "Sarah" came in unannounced and interrupted us. Sarah was young, in her twenties, and cute. She said, "I'm so sorry to break this up. Not because it isn't sweet, but it's time for bloodwork and your dinner will be coming soon. Tonight it's meatloaf and baked potato."

I tried not to laugh at Trey's reaction. "Yum, Jess, any chance of getting take-out from Eddie's Tacos?"

Sarah waved her finger in the air. "That's a definite no-no. Nothing spicy for you at least for the next few days."

Trey gave me a hug and responded, "The only spice I need is my best gal."

Best gal. I liked the sounds of that. I got off his lap, a little embarrassed, and gently touched his shoulder. "Trey, it's probably a good idea if we leave now considering you have lab work and dinner." I smiled. "Sorry you're not having Eddie's Tacos, but you can still have my melted chocolate." I opened my other hand to show him what had become of my truffle. "That's how your kisses melt my heart. Besides, it's almost five thirty and I should get dinner for the boys. The light contest is about to begin."

I grabbed a tissue to wipe my hand, held up Sam's leash and signaled to him. "Come on big guy, give Trey a kiss."

Trey looked bummed out. "Sure you don't want to stay? I'm sure they make extra meatloaf."

"We do," Sarah responded, "and you are more than welcome to stay. Some guests come after work to visit our patients and we want to help accommodate their visits as much as possible even serving dinner when needed."

I smiled at her. "Thanks, but I don't want to wear out my welcome. Besides, as nice an offer as that is, I promised to bring my neighbors dinner from Eddie's for helping me with a project."

"Jess, you could never wear out your welcome," Trey said. Sarah left briefly and returned with a small cardboard box. "I'm sending these cupcakes home with you. I hope you'll enjoy them."

"Thank you. I love chocolate cupcakes. Well, anything chocolate and they're so festive," I responded as she filled my take home box.

As soon as she left, Trey took my hand and wouldn't let go. I had to remind him. "Trey, we really have to go. They have to take tests and then there's that meatloaf dinner."

He rubbed fake tears from his eyes. "I'll miss you two every minute until tomorrow. Come here boy, let me give you another hug." Trey slapped his legs and Sam understood that meant to jump up and lick him. He then turned to me as I grabbed Sam's leash. "I hope you don't find me too bold, but this afternoon felt like our first date. I mean even though we're in a rehab center."

I paused. "Funny you should say that. It felt like one to me as well."

Trey had a devilish look in his eyes. He stood and with the help of his walker came over to me. He grabbed me by my waist and pulled me in to him for a sweet kiss.

Even though his kiss surprised me, I wondered if he had any idea how much I loved it. When our lips parted, I wanted him to know so I kissed him back! Oh, well, what did I have to lose? When in Rome...

I looked into his gorgeous blue eyes as he still held me in his arms and asked. "Are you ready for another goodnight kiss?" Before I could answer, he pressed his lips against mine before running his soft kisses down to the base of my neck. Chills ran up my spine. I wanted more. He sensed that and caressed me as we stood there in our own romantic coma. Then came the fireworks, he gave me the most romantic goodnight kiss I've ever had. He deepened the kiss and we held that kiss for a long while until someone entering the room interrupted our passion. It was a quite surprised lab attendant. He cleared his throat, I guess as a signal to stop.

"It's time for bloodwork. Miss, if you'd like to come back afterwards, there is a guest lounge with coffee and cookies past the front desk. Now all human and animal guests must leave the room so I can do this."

We took the hint. I picked up my cupcake box, grabbed Sam's leash, and blew Trey a kiss. "We'll talk later. I'll let you know what happens with the contest. Be good."

"Always," he quipped, "how can I not be?"

I smiled. "See you tomorrow. This has been a magical afternoon for me."

"It has for me too, my lovely lady. See you then. Bye buddy."

I could tell by the lab tech's expression he was relieved we were finally leaving so he could finish Trey's tests. Sam stopped short in the doorway and looked back at Trey wagging his tail. I gave his leash a tug and I left for Eddie's Tacos a lot more smitten.

Sam and I were already too late to try and get home in time for the judging. With traffic and my stop at Eddie's, we'll be lucky to make it home by six thirty. I was happy Trey felt better and comfortable with his new surroundings.

I'd better not dawdle too long about calling in my order else we'll be even later. "Hi. Jessica Munroe, here. I'd like to pick up six tacos and three steak fajita dinners. I'll be by in about thirty minutes."

Eddie, who had a distinct accent responded, "No problem, Señorita Jess. Everything will be ready. Hey, I heard you have a new dog. A big one. That's great. Everyone knows how much you miss Mazy."

Wow! Local gossip must have already substituted Sam's

arrival for my change in lipstick shades. Those island ladies sure stay busy updating information. I had to tell him. "Eddie, he's not mine. I'm taking care of him for his owner who's in the hospital."

Order confirmed, we drove through holiday traffic straight to Eddie's. I drove into the drive-thru. A server handed my bag to me via the take-out window.

"Is that a dog or a horse?" she asked. I smiled. "Sam is a dog. Thank you."

I took my bag and left before more curious staffers came to the window to check Sam out. My watch read six fifteen.

I drove behind slow holiday light onlookers to the south end of the island. The entire island was lit with holiday cheer. Almost every house we passed was decorated and glowing. When I turned down my side street, I looked up to see the sky lit like an alien vehicle had just landed. Could that be my house? Sam saw it as well and barked. We passed three houses with normal holiday displays before I heard loud Christmas music. Turning into my driveway, I needed sunglasses and ear plugs, but sitting in the midst of this LED winter wonderland made me feel like a kid again. I'm sure Terry and Rich were happy that I left them alone. I looked around. They added to the already over decorated display. Even so, I can't help but love them and what they did for me. Besides the music, they had color wheels projecting designs of snowflakes across the front of my house and a giant inflatable flamingo wearing a Santa hat sat positioned in the center of my small yard. Where did they find the extra room amidst all these lights? And where and when did they get that flamingo?

They must have seen my headlights approach because they ran out of my house to my car. "Jess, you're late. It's almost seven but no bother. How do you like the new stuff? Come, get out, and walk around."

I wanted to take a closer look because these two wonderful guys did all this for me to make my holiday open house extra special. Surrounded by all the sparkling decorations, I felt like the ghost of Christmas present had just paid me a visit. I grabbed Sam's leash, handed Terry my bag from Eddie's and my cupcakes, and walked Sam by the road to do his business before wafting back mesmerized by that maze of beautiful decorations.

"This is so beautiful. The pink and white lights are soft yet cheerful. Thank you for doing all this even if we don't win."

Rich answered as Terry brought our dinner inside. "Oh, but surprise. I just found out a couple of minutes ago that we did win. A few minutes after seven, a judge called my cell which I left as our contact number on the application and said they had never seen a light show like ours in all their years of judging. They went on to say congratulations. You won!"

Oh, my gosh! I couldn't believe it. I jumped up and down in excitement; Sam followed my lead. After we all calmed down, I gave Rich a hug and Sam gave his face a lick. Rich laughed, "Okay, let's eat before Eddie's magic gets cold."

"Right." I replied as Sam and I went into the kitchen. Terry had set the table, poured some wine, and filled Sam's dishes. I had to give Terry a hug as well. I told him. "I can't believe we won. I feel like a snow princess in Florida of course."

Terry held my chair for me making me feel like royalty adding "You are our snow princess in Florida. Now your highness, let's have our royal feast and celebrate our victory."

We filled our plates and chowed down. "There's just one more surprise," Terry added. "You will be awarded a trophy."

I gushed. "A trophy? I've never won a trophy before. I thought they were reserved for cool people."

"Well, to be a snow princess, you have to be cool. So much so our local news photographer called and wants to photograph you holding your trophy in front of town hall at nine tomorrow morning. He wants to make deadline for the

Christmas issue of The Island News. After which, he said the town will host a ceremony awarding the trophies."

"Wow. That's great. I can be there and maybe Sam can come with me."

I laughed, excited by the entire evening. Sam loved the sounds of my happiness.

"I can't wait to tell Trey."

Rich was happy to ask, "Now's who's ready for dessert? Cherries à la mode."

Of course we all were. An incredible dessert for an incredible evening.

CHAPTER 11

The very first thing I did after returning from the town hall ceremony was to call Trey. "Hey," he answered. "How's my gorgeous trophy winner?"

"You can't believe how happy I am at this moment. I can't wait for Christmas. I invited Terry and Rich to come with me to the trophy ceremony since they did the lion's share of the work, but they refused to take a photo with me for the paper. They said, 'You and Sam are much cuter.'"

Trey chuckled. "You sounded pretty hyped last night when you told me you won, but I'm happy to say, this morning you sound even more so."

"I am so very happy. Anyway, I'm getting ahead of myself. The Town Hall allows well behaved pets so Sam came with us. The outside of the hall was decorated with silver and gold garlands. Three small artificial Christmas trees decorated with gift cards donated by our local merchants were placed on the trophy table outside for the ceremony.

"I met with the news photographer earlier at nine and he photographed me holding my beautiful trophy with Sam next to me of course. My trophy had a tall red and white metal candy cane attached to a wooden base where my brass name plate will go."

I took a deep breath. "There was one large tree and two smaller ones. The mayor started the ceremony by wishing all attendees a happy holiday and a huge thank you to all who participated in this event. Santa then came on stage to announce the winners. He announced my house as the first place winner and the mayor handed me my trophy, a paper proclamation, and the biggest tree loaded with gift cards. I could barely hold everything.

"Rich came running up to grab my tree and proclamation before I dropped them. That was so much fun! Sam remained by my side and was so good, Santa gave him a pet. Cameras clicked before the mayor announced the two runners-up. I felt guilty being up there alone with Sam because I wanted Rich and Terry by my side. A reporter from the Ft. Myers newspaper took us aside afterwards to take our photo for their Sunday edition. I held my trophy in the air. Terry and Rich cheered from the sidelines."

Trey laughed. "Congratulations once more. I already told you your island knows how to celebrate. Now that you're a big media star, will you ever visit me again?"

"You know I will, but there's more. We had a reception afterwards inside the hall with finger sandwiches, salads, and all kinds of chips, crackers, cheeses, and homemade dips. Everyone thought we were finished eating until they wheeled out a huge red and white cake decorated with a candy cane made of frosting on top. Oh, my gosh! It was so good. I can still taste it. Lucky I had few cookies for Sam in my pocket so he wouldn't feel left out. The three winners had our photo taken together in front of the cake for the town's website before it was cut. Terry and Rich held onto Sam. Good thing I wore a nice dress. After all the celebrating finished, so many islanders came over to congratulate us. I've never experienced anything like it. Terry and Rich were so happy I was the one receiving all of the attention and Sam loved all the petting he received as well."

Trey chuckled. "You are a big media star!"

I laughed. "I guess, especially since the mayor came over to inform me that a reporter from our local TV channel wanted to come to my house tonight and interview me while the lights were lit. Of course I said 'Yes'. The TV reporter is coming right after five thirty this evening. I asked Rich and Terry to come and participate as well. So this media star will have to visit you in the middle of the afternoon today. I hope that fits in with your test schedule? Wish I had a piece of that candy cane cake to bring you. I'm letting you know ahead of time. No tempting with meatloaf."

I heard Trey laugh harder this time. "This afternoon will be great. I love to see you anytime, besides tonight they're having spaghetti and meatballs."

I was quick to respond. "No tempting with that either. I'll have to do something with my hair for TV but even so Sam and I will leave soon hoping to get to you around one thirty. We'll have to leave by three thirty because of all the traffic."

Trey responded, "You, my fair lady, are on. Oh and please bring some more of those chocolatey kisses. I can't wait."

Our call ended, I brushed my hair and put it up in a French bun with my mother's beautiful antique hair clip she brought back from Paris. For a hippie, she sure had classy taste. I already had on a cranberry dress for the ceremony so I'll touch up my hair's loose ends and my make-up after I get home from visiting Trey. Sam did his business and hopped into my back seat. We were ready to visit Trey.

After we arrived, Skip greeted us and hugged Sam. He went into his top drawer and took out a cellophane wrapped frosted dog bone. "Buddy, this is for you. You are my favorite visiting dog." Sam just loved it, but I took it to show Trey. "Skip, thank you. That's so sweet. I'm going to show this to Mr. M. before Sam enjoys it."

We both pranced down to Trey's room. Sitting in the recliner, he greeted us with open arms. Sam tugged at his leash so I let him go running right into Trey's arms. After getting licked to pieces, he took one look at me and wolf whistled.

"You look beautiful in that dress. Cranberry is your color and your hair looks great. I guess I've never seen you this dressed up. You should do it more often. When I get out of here, I'm going to take you to the fanciest restaurants I know and give you more reasons to dress up."

I grinned. "Now don't get too cocky. I'm happy with a burger and fries or conch fritters. Odd, you have no tests today?"

"I lucked out. They were all scheduled for early this morning."

I held up Sam's new cookie. "Skip bought this for him. Sam's been so good I'm going to give it to him now." Since I had Sam's undivided attention, I opened the wrapping and gave him the treat. Drool dripped down both side of his jowls.

"He's a lucky dog. After all this excitement with you, life with me will seem boring," Trey said holding his arms out this time for me. I closed the door leaving it open just a crack and sat next to him on the arm of the chair. I leaned in and gave him a "hello" kiss. "He loves you so much he could never be bored."

He smiled. "Your kisses make my heart race a mile a minute." He winked. "Take it easy on me I have physical therapy first thing tomorrow morning, but I don't care so how about another kiss?"

I was more than happy to oblige. I placed my big bag on the floor next to my chair. Sam was too busy with Skip's treat to put his nose inside of it. Trey looked at him, so content chewing.

"Sam is celebrating his new stardom along with yours. That's a pretty big treat. Think it'll spoil his dinner?"

"Doubt it," I replied. "He eats like a horse. I try to keep his food and treats to a moderate level so he doesn't gain any weight, but today he gets to celebrate first class."

I pulled out two holiday chocolate kisses from my purse. "And we do too. Now Red or Green?" I asked Trey.

"Red of course," he responded as I handed him the right color foil wrapper. "Ready. One. Two. Three. Unwrap."

He gently tugged on my arm to interfere with my progress before pulling me over to him. He had his chocolate unwrapped and in his mouth before giving me a deep kiss. Deep enough, so I could taste the dark melted chocolate. Our kiss lasted for quite a while until Sam got up wanting to get in the act and licked the sides of our faces.

"Anyone ever tell you you're a snake?" I asked.

"As a divorce attorney, I believe I've heard the phase once or twice from the opposition. Besides, always bet on red. It's a hot fast color, Green is calm and cool."

I opened my chocolate and put it in my mouth before instigating our next hot kiss. I could get used to this. When our lips parted, Trey squeezed my shoulder. "You are the sweetest and cutest media star I know. When will they air this interview? I'd love to see it."

I was happy to respond. "Tonight on the eleven o'clock local news and they will feature us as their lead holiday story tomorrow on the five, six, and eleven o'clock news. Fret not, I'll still visit tomorrow. You are stuck with me. I'll record the interviews, providing I look good and sound coherent."

Trey smiled. "I was hoping you'd visit tomorrow night. I have something extra special planned for us so please record your interview. I can't wait to watch it."

Extra special? What now? I wondered as he continued. "I want you to have dinner with me. Before you say 'no', let me assure you that it won't be meatloaf or tuna casserole. I received approval from my dietician to order dinner from The Island Steak House so I did and ordered appetizers, salad, and dinner. The only complication is we have to eat at five in order to keep my meds and tests on schedule."

I was flabbergasted. "The Island Steak House? That's always been a bit above my budget. Sounds great. What can I bring?"

He looked at me with a sweet softness in his eyes. "You and Sam are my guests. The Steakhouse even makes special doggie bags, but you can get dressed up like you are now. You look stunning."

I blushed. Couldn't help it. Jake never noticed things like that. "I can do that," I answered. "It's a date. Wow! Almost a real one. We'll be here by four-thirty." I kissed his forehead before getting Sam's leash ready to leave and do my interview.

Sam and I arrived home about an hour before my big media debut. Surprise, Terry and Rich cheered us from my front porch as we drove in. "We came over to make sure your display was perfect for TV."

I raced inside and gave Sam dinner before going to my room to fix my make-up and hair. All that kissing can do a number on a lady's appearance. I looked in my dresser mirror. "You look stunning" echoed in my mind. So far, I have been careful not to fall in love with Trey. What woman wouldn't fall for him? He's handsome, sensitive, intelligent, and has gorgeous blue eyes. The sensitive and handsome parts appealed to me the most. I fell for Sam at first bark. I know it's going to be tough if I have to say goodbye to them. Back to my hair and make-up as I redid my up do and placed that beautiful comb on the side of my hair that would show best on TV. By the time I went back to my kitchen, Terry had walked Sam, groomed him for TV, and put his jingle bells back on. "You both are going to hit this interview out of the park."

"Terry, I don't feel right not having you both interviewed with me. You and Rich deserve all the credit for this."

"We're not photogenic," Rich, who just came in the kitchen, laughed. "We'll compromise. You can thank us for assisting you and we'll stand on the porch in the background and wave. Ask the reporter if that's possible. How's that?"

"Better," I said as I heard a vehicle pull up in front of the house. I went to the front door and looked out the window to see the TV van pulling up. It was five thirty. With the sound of one automated click, my winter wonderland turned on along with music and animated falling snow shooting from color wheels. There was a knock on my front door. I made a sign for Sam to be quiet, grabbed my trophy, and answered the door. "Hi, I'm Jess and this is Sam."

The pretty reporter dressed in a navy blue suit smiled when she saw him. "I'm Tanya. How about we do this on your front lawn with all those amazing lights in the background? The viewers who can't make it to the Beach will love to see what you've done. My video photographer Ned is outside filming them now so we can run his shots as a promo. I promise my questions will be short but fun."

"Thanks. I appreciate that. I have two neighbors who helped me with this project. Before we finish, can I have them wave and give them some credit?" I asked.

"Of course, but I'll do that briefly at the end of the interview. After all, you are my star," she replied. "Now let's go get set up. Is this young man coming with us?"

"Yes, he is if that's all right?" I asked Tanya as she held her hand out for Sam to sniff. "That's great! He's so sweet for a big guy. Just follow me and we'll get you miked up."

We followed her to stand smack dab in the center of my walkway with all the lights surrounding us. Sam had his jingle bell collar on. Terry and Rich had already lowered the volume on the music before Tanya arrived. Ned clipped a microphone to the front of my dress, and we were ready on three. Kind of like chocolates, a happy thought that lessened my anxiety about being on TV.

Tanya looked at me and nodded as the young man held up his fingers and counted down. "Ready on three. One, Two, Three…" His hand shot to Tanya.

"Hello Southwest Florida. Tanya Redstone reporting from beautiful Hibiscus Island, all lit up ready to celebrate the holidays. Standing next to me are island resident Jessica Monroe and her buddy Sam, whose house, as you can see by our amazing backdrop, won first place in the Beach Holiday Light Festival. Jess, how long have you lived on the island and what inspired you to enter the contest this year?"

I smiled and looked into the camera. "I was born here and lived here my entire life. This year, because of personal reasons, I needed some holiday cheer to get me in the mood to celebrate. That made me think of all the others who, for whatever reason, needed some extra cheer as well, so we did this for them and everyone else to enjoy."

"That's a very nice thought from someone your fellow islanders dub as a guardian angel. I hear you bake Christmas cookies for the senior center every year, taking them over yourself, and you are taking care of Sam here until his owner gets out of the hospital."

"Yes. I try to work on as many community projects as my job as an associate editor for a national travel magazine allows during the year. I enjoy helping others very much and Sam is such a joy to take care of, especially since I lost my own dog Mazy a couple months back."

Tanya winked. "Jess, you look strong, but did you hang all of these lights by yourself?"

I loved that question. "No, I had the help of my two wonderful neighbors, Terry and Rich." That was their cue to wave from my front porch.

Tanya signaled for a close up of them. She then finished the interview adding. "Thank you Jess and Sam for doing this interview. It certainly cheered up my holiday spirit, this being my first year away from family and old friends. This is Tanya Redstone signing out from Jessica's magical beach winter wonderland."

Ned gave a signal and Tanya said, "That's it. We'll air this tonight at eleven and as you know tomorrow and now Sunday at five, six and eleven as well. Great interview. Great dog."

She gave Sam a hug as I asked, "Did you mean what you said about being alone over the holidays? For obvious reasons, I didn't want to mention this on air, but I have an annual open house for islanders with nowhere or no one to celebrate the holiday. It's on Christmas Eve and starts at five thirty. You are more than welcome to come and bring a guest if you'd like."

Tanya smiled. "What they say about you being an angel is true. Isn't it? Thank you. I just might see you there."

Once the TV van left, Terry and Rich invited me over to their house for dinner. What would I do without these two? Sam and I followed. Rich made his famous lasagna that he kept warm in the oven and had some of Sam's food in a big dish alongside one with drinking water. As soon we got back home, I called Trey, excited to tell him about our interview and asking him to watch.

I didn't think anything could top last night for excitement but seeing Trey tonight and experience what he planned may just surpass that. That morning, I worked on a submission I received for our January edition and wrapped small gifts for my party that was creeping up way too fast. I couldn't believe all the phone calls I received congratulating me on my interview. I was surprised when I received one from Jake.

The holiday edition of the Beach newspaper came out today with the photo of me, Sam, and my trophy enlarged and plastered on the front page. Terry picked up six extra copies when he went to the grocery store so I could send them out to family and friends who didn't have internet.

My sister might like one and I can take one to Trey tonight. Trey, I can't even think about that man without a big smile bursting across my face. I have to stop that, especially since I've already had my heart broken once this year. I can't let go of my fear that my heart might get crushed again.

I decided to search my closet for the perfect dress to wear to dinner. Aha. The royal blue wrap around. Royal blue is my color or so Rich tells me whenever I wear it because of my dark hair and brown eyes. Trey liked my hair yesterday so I'll wear it up like that today.

I looked at my watch. 1:00 p.m., a bit early to for me to get ready but I can start with Sam. The doorbell interrupted my thoughts. I opened the door to find a delivery from the Beach Florist left on my front door mat. It was a small box, easy to grab, so I took it inside. I opened it to find the most beautiful corsage of pink roses and white baby's breath. A note read, "For my beautiful date. I can't wait to see you tonight."

A corsage. How romantic, albeit sort of cheesy, but sweet too! I haven't had one since my high school prom. The blue dress is a definite since the pink roses will go perfectly with it. I put the flowers in my fridge and turned to Sam. I knew I better get him ready before getting dressed myself.

Sam finished. I put on that blue dress and took one last look in my bedroom mirror before returning to the kitchen for my flowers. Just as I was about to pin on my corsage, there was a knock on the kitchen door. Really? Sometimes I feel like I live in Grand Central Station. I looked out the window. It was Terry.

He barreled his way in to give me some advice. "You know, maybe you should leave Sam here with us. You might come home later than you expect, and you don't need Sam interrupting any romantic moment if you get my drift."

Terry took one look at me. "Wow. Ooh la la! We always told you royal blue is your color. Is that a corsage? From Trey? How nice. He really does like you. Let me help you pin that on sweetie and take care of Sam tonight."

Terry picked up the flowers and pinned them on just right. I touched his hand. "Thank you. I would have fumbled with the pins. Won't Trey miss Sam?"

Terry chuckled. "Trust me, honey. The way you look now, he'll only have eyes for you tonight."

Terrible thing to say, but Terry is one of the few people in my life who gives me good advice, besides the smell of steak may be too much for my furry friend. "All right, I think you may be right. Please remember, not too many treats for Sam. I have human treats for you in the freezer like ice cream pops along with cheese popcorn in the pantry."

"Don't worry about us. We'll be fine," Terry reassured me.

I took a deep breath hoping I made the right decision and left to see Trey.

CHAPTER 12

I felt so guilty about leaving Sam home I decided to call Trey while still parked in my driveway. Trey surprised me and agreed with my decision.

"That's perfect. That way I'll have more time to spend with you."

His desire for us to spend time together alone made me feel special. After all, he did meet Sam first. When I walked into the front entrance of rehab without Sam, Skip became concerned. "Is Sam all right? I have another holiday cookie for him. Look it's shaped like a candy cane." He held it up for me to see before taking a long look at me. "Wow, do you look pretty."

He sounded a little surprised. I wondered how bad I must look normally. "Skip, Sam will be here tomorrow. My neighbors wanted to spoil him tonight. Please save that wonderful candy cane shaped cookie for him to enjoy then."

Skip appeared happier. "I will," he responded placing the cookie back in his drawer. I left the front desk and walked down Trey's hallway. The closer I got to his room the louder free flowing Christmas carols became. When I turned to enter his room, I noticed an iPod on the dresser playing those happy sounds. Trey, seated in his big chair, was dressed not in his usual shorts but casual tan pants and an emerald green collared dress shirt. Bet he was happy he didn't have to wear a suit and tie like he did for work. On the beach, his current outfit would be considered formal wear.

Trey saw me and stood. His captivating blue eyes followed me into his room. I lost my breath when I saw how handsome he looked but caught myself after he turned the tables on me. "You look amazing," he told me. "That blue dress is sexy."

Heat flushed through my face. My cheeks were on fire so I knew I blushed. Wanting to change the subject, I looked down at my flowers. "Thank you for this lovely corsage. It makes me feel young and special."

Trey walked over to me and whispered in my ear. "You are very special to me." He held my hands, planting a gentle kiss on my lips.

"Please come into my winter wonderland. I watched you on TV last night and will again tonight at eleven. You were great. A real natural. So now after seeing you on TV, I can't get enough of you."

I looked around at his room. Tinsel garlands in red and green hung around the window frame. White twinkling lights surrounded his dresser mirror. The room lights had been dimmed and a silver tinsel tree lit with multi-colored mini lights sat next to his iPod.

A square shaped table on wheels, like the kind a hospital food server uses to deliver meals, was in the center of the room covered by a red tablecloth and set for two with holiday dishes in a holly and ivy pattern. I felt like I had walked into George Bailey's dining room at Christmas. White mums and red poinsettias in an emerald green ceramic pot served as the centerpiece. I was so surprised by what he had done, I could barely speak.

Trey walked me over to one of the chairs and asked. "Do you like my surprise?"

I smiled. "I sure do."

My eyes circled his room again. "How did you do all of this?"

"I have my secrets," he answered. "Everyone on staff in this wing was in on our date. Now please have a seat and tell me about your day."

Trey, the perfect gentleman, pulled the chair back for me. I thought, my day? No one ever asks me about my day so I began. "Well, since you asked. I know you watched my interview. I hope I didn't appear too excited or naive."

He smiled. "Too cute maybe, but that's what makes you so watchable."

I continued trying hard for my heart not to melt from looking into his eyes. "The Beach paper had my cottage, Sam, and I on the front cover today. I brought you a copy if you'd like one."

I pulled the paper out of my large purse and handed it to him. "Besides that, I began to wrap the small gifts I give to my open house guests. While I was wrapping, there was a knock on my door and a delivery came with these lovely flowers." I smelled my roses. "Pink roses are my favorite. I guess that's it in a nutshell."

Trey looked playful as he perused my front page photo. "You know you never sent me an invite to your open house. I guess Sam and I aren't invited."

"I thought you'd be going home back to town by then. I'd love for you to come and have the three of us celebrate together. The open house starts at five thirty at 886 Pelican Road on the south end of the island," I answered.

Trey laughed. "I think after sending two deliveries, I know your address by now. Well, we accept and will be there with bells on. Sam already has his so I'll have to get some for myself."

He kissed my forehead and put the newspaper on his dresser. "Would you care for some eggnog to kick off our celebration along with assorted cheeses and crackers? Since rehab restricts alcohol, I have to apologize for the lack of rum in the eggnog."

Wow he was so classy he could make a rehab room feel like the Ritz. I smiled and answered, "yes" as he buzzed for an attendant. A woman wearing an Island Steak House uniform came in with two glasses of egg nog and a tray of assorted cheese and crackers that looked like it came from a deli not the rehab kitchen. There were also carrot and celery sticks and a creamy dip.

She handed each of us a glass of eggnog and placed the tray in the center of the table. We already had canapé dishes and napkins. Trey looked at the server. "Thanks, Nancy." She smiled and left. Trey raised his glass. "To a very Merry Christmas for the three of us. Even though Sam is not with us tonight, he'll be with us then."

"To the three of us," I repeated still in a bit of shock at all of this. We enjoyed the fabulous selection of cheeses and dip as he began to open up about his plans. "My physical therapist thinks I should be strong enough to leave by Christmas Eve. Good thing I worked out before the accident."

"Good thing," I added mentally drooling over his muscular physique while feeling sad at the thought I might lose both of them. He then told me about his rental condo on the south end of the island and how he'll stay there once released from here. "I've never used it because I always tried to keep it rented. Now might be the perfect time to do so. It's on the beach side of the road not too far from you. I or should I say we plan on spending Christmas Eve with you."

My mind swirled with happiness thinking I sure hope so. Nancy checked in to see if we needed anything. Trey winked. "We're ready to start dinner anytime you're ready for us."

She looked at me. "Say weren't you on the late news last night with an adorable dog and a million holiday lights? You were great by the way. If I get out of work a little early one night before Christmas, I'm going to drive up and down the island to look at all the decorations."

"Thanks Nancy. I appreciate that," I responded as she picked up the trays of snacks. It took mere minutes before Nancy returned with a smaller rolling hospital food cart. There was a large bowl of Caesar salad with two plates and salad forks along with a basket of mixed rolls and butter. She filled our salad plates and placed one roll on each bread dish before leaving as quickly as she came.

"Trey, I still want to know. How on earth did you arrange all of this?" I asked as I took the first bite of my salad.

"I told Sarah, my nurse, that I met a pretty wonderful lady and I'd like to show her how special she was to me. I asked her to speak to the rehab food manager to see if I could have food brought in from a local restaurant and what restraints he had on the delivery. Once the manager agreed, Island Steakhouse sent a menu to my room. I just needed my selection for this evening to be approved by the dietician. He said 'yes' his only problem being he couldn't have any. We are dining on Island Steakhouse food only in rehab. To show my gratitude for helping me, I offered to contribute to the staff holiday party they're having next week."

I sat back in disbelief. Even in rehab, he's a mover and shaker. He smiled at me. "Now let's dig into our salads. They look great and those rolls smell amazing. Sourdough and wheat I think."

The rolls were warm and delicious especially after melting the butter patties shaped like flowers on them. The Caesar salad tasted so fresh like it was just tossed. We finished the first course; Trey used his magic buzzer to call that rolling cart. Nancy came back into our room again.

I looked into his eyes. "This is truly incredible. You made eating in a rehab room like dining in a dream."

Nancy cleared our salad plates before handing us each a steak knife frowned upon in most hospitals but I'm sure the dietician here had Trey cleared to use them. Nancy placed two dinner plates in front of us before serving us from her cart. She placed fillet minion, baked stuffed potato, asparagus, and a skewer of broiled island shrimp on each plate. She left two small dishes, one with Béarnaise sauce and the other with ketchup. Unbelievable. The char broiled steak and shrimp smelled so delicious my stomach went wild.

Before she left, Nancy turned to me and whispered in my ear. "I hope you know what a lucky lady you are. Mr. Trey went to a great deal of trouble to put this together."

I agreed. "Thank you Nancy for helping with all of this. I do know. He makes me feel like a queen." Nancy touched my arm before leaving with the cart.

Trey announced, "We couldn't have any wine so I hope Root Beer and water work."

I laughed. "That's perfect. I love Root Beer. How long did all the decorations take? They weren't here yesterday."

"Ah my lady, never ask a wizard how he does his magic. Let's just say I work like Santa and have lots of elves." He laughed as did Nancy who came back in with our drinks just in time to hear his answer.

My steak melted in my mouth and the creamy Béarnaise sauce was to die for. And that pink juicy shrimp! I could see by Trey's expressions he agreed. "I wonder if they're open Christmas Day."

I answered. "They always have been. Christmas is the official start of our tourist season."

Trey responded in between bites. "Great. We'll celebrate Christmas Eve at your house and Christmas Day dinner at The Island Steakhouse. I'll ask Nancy to make us a reservation for 4:00 p.m. Does that work for you?"

Still not willing to believe this was happening to me, I didn't know what to say. Will he still want to see me once he's out of rehab? But I answered hoping his invite will come true.

"Four is fine. That's very nice of you. I've heard they have a huge salad bar and it's very good."

"Salad bar sounds great even for a carnivore. I'm not being nice." He laughed. "I really want to spend Christmas with you. I'm a terrible cook and I don't want you to cook especially after you've spent so much time helping me get better. So Island Steak House is the best I can offer. We'll bring Sam a tremendous doggie bag. I ordered one for him tonight too."

We continued to enjoy our dinners. How could anyone not? I don't usually eat at The Island Steak House since it's over budget for an associate editor so I genuinely appreciated Trey's treat.

We talked during dinner like we were on a real date. Trey suggested. "Why don't we tell each other a little about our pasts?"

I volunteered to start. "Since I'm the more boring of the two of us, I'll begin. I grew up on Hibiscus Island in the same house I'm living in now. I inherited the cottage after my parents died in a plane crash coming home from a Caribbean vacation. They left the property to both my sister and I, but my sister turned the deed over to me since she was well-off, married, and already settled in a home of her own. I remember my sister never really liked the Beach. Trust me, an editor and contributing writer could never afford property on Hibiscus Island now. At the time, I had just graduated from college, the University of Florida, and not yet financially on my feet. I grew up on the island and had a lot of happy memories and many friends, who still live here, so owning my Beach cottage meant a great deal to me."

He interrupted, "I can't wait to see it."

I smiled, "I'd love for you to see it. It's not sophisticated or large, but I love living on a canal where I can watch manatees and dolphin. Anyway my first job was writing obituaries for a county newspaper. As my writing improved I wrote more feature articles especially on travel and leisure. I got up my courage and submitted one to a national online travel magazine. My parents loved to travel and as a child went on some pretty terrific adventures even though at the time I didn't think they were. I am now an associate editor for that same magazine."

Trey sat back and listened. "Sounds like you are not only good but enjoy what you do. Who knows, maybe the next step in your writing career will be a novel? Where can I find your articles? I'd like to read them."

"I've got some print-outs at home. Since you don't have your computer here, I'll bring some in tomorrow to help pass the time from boredom. The magazine comes out monthly and is called *Dream Travel*. Now enough about me, it's your turn. Where did you grow up?"

Trey hedged a little. "Our conversation makes me uncomfortable. As a lawyer, I'm usually the one asking the questions, not answering them. I grew up in downtown Ft. Myers. As you can tell by all the buildings that have my last name on them, my grandparents were politically active and very charitable. They were life-long philanthropists so after their death, my parents wanted to continue in their tradition but on a smaller scale since they didn't have my grandparents' stock portfolio. Trust me, my parents are very generous and help as many charitable groups as they can. They still live in town when they are not out of the country doing missionary work which is where they are now. I have one sister, Gina, who cares about nothing else but her fashion designer career in New York City. She's cold and doesn't care about anyone else but herself. I always wondered if she came from the same human gene pool as I did or if she was adopted."

"Being different is not unusual. My sister and I are polar opposites," I interjected.

He chuckled. "Not as opposite as Gina and I are. Anyway please don't hold my affluent upbringing against me. My parents sent me to out of state private schools and after graduation I was lucky enough to get into Cornell where I received my undergraduate degree before attending law school there. My father was a doctor and was disappointed I didn't follow in his footsteps but has accepted my career choice and is proud of my success. My law partner is amazing. He's smart and empathetic and our clients adore him. I guess they like me too. I try to carry on the family tradition of giving and take one pro bono case a month. Lots of people need help. I still live in town, not in my family homestead since my parents are still there when they're not helping doctors without borders. They are in Africa now. They didn't come back after my accident because my doctors here kept them informed. After I woke up, Dad called and told me they had tickets ready in case I needed them here with me. Anyway I live in a modern high-rise condo on the river that allows pets. Sam is my roomie and as you already know, I love him."

I sighed. "Sure sounds like you lived a charmed life. We sure have had different life experiences so far and yet here we are together."

Nancy came back into the room and noticed our clean plates. "Dinner must have been great. I can't find a crumb on either plate. Are you two ready for a wonderful holiday dessert? This next course is complements of this facility's chef."

Trey answered. "Sounds great. That's a nice surprise. I didn't order dessert, but I still have room for some. Nancy would you check on a dinner reservation for two at the Steak House on Christmas Day at four? If they're open and can accommodate our reservation, please confirm it before you leave."

"I will," she said loading our empty dinner plates onto her cart. She returned with a small square layer cake. It had white creamy frosting with red and green decorations in the design of a tree. It was almost too pretty to cut but when she did, I saw dark chocolate frosting between two layers of devil's food cake.

Chocolate has always been my middle name. I salivated just looking at the cake. Nancy cut two pieces and placed each one on dishes she brought in along with dessert forks adding, "The staff asked me to tell you how much they appreciate your donation to help with their party and hope this special cake will show you how much. When I return to pick up the dessert dishes, I'll let you know about your reservation."

"Thank you. I'll have to thank the staff for this totally unexpected but wonderful surprise as well," Trey responded.

I couldn't help it. I dug right into that cake even after that huge dinner. Not lady like I know but who could resist dark chocolate? We cleaned our cake plates.

I chuckled, "You're spoiling me like you do Sam. Once spoiled, you know there's no turning back."

Trey shrugged his shoulder. "Maybe spoiling those I love is something I enjoy."

Love? I wondered if that was his meds talking. My facial expressions must have given my thoughts away. He continued, "Yes, Jess, love. I know it's been less than a month since we met, and I was in a coma so hearing the word 'love' at this point must sound silly. Look I'm trying to make sense here. It seems that ever since you came into my life, I have a sense of joy, a sense of laughter, a sense of freedom with emotions I've never felt with anyone else. Just your presence makes my temperature rise, my heart beat faster, and my lips quiver, anxious to meet yours. I'm not crazy and this is not a reaction to my medication. This is plain and simple what happens when you fall in love. You must know I'm right. You must have fallen in love before with someone special. Granted, it might not have worked out then, but maybe that's fate telling us we were meant to be together now. Jess I love you."

He stood and walked to where I was sitting. Taking hold

of my hands, he helped me stand and threw his muscular arms around me. My heart throbbed; my body trembled, as my lips quivered to meet his. He held my face in his hands and gave me a long and passionate kiss. I became lost in our passion as he deepened the kiss. My muscles weakened and I melted in his arms. We were so caught up in our sensual feelings we were unaware of the world around us. So unaware that we did not hear a faint knock on the door. The knock got louder.

"Oh. Please excuse me," Nancy said trying, I'm sure, to make believe she didn't see us. "I'll be quick and clear the plates. Your reservation for Christmas dinner is all set. I'll be your server and will leave my card on the dresser in case there's something special you would like to order. I'd like to thank you Mr. Musgrove for your generous tip and will leave now."

She picked up our place settings, pushed the large hospital cart into the hall, and closed the door. We were alone again. Still standing, Trey pulled me closer. "How about another one of those wonderful kisses? Hmmm, maybe two? They're going to kick you out of here in about an hour at eight-thirty."

I laughed. Just as our lips met, someone knocked again.

"Pre-ordered doggy bag for Sam. Nancy left it for me to deliver to you," Nurse Sarah said opening the door slowly. "And here's the rest of the cake for Jess to take home. Skip wanted to send Sam this festive biscuit with Jess as well."

Trey looked pleased. "Feels like Christmas already and the staff likes you and Sam as much as I do."

I took the two small packages from her. "Thank you and please thank everyone who made tonight so special for us."

She left and closed the door almost all the way on her way out. I placed the cake box, the doggie bag, and the biscuit on the dresser. "Now," I asked Trey. "Where were we?" He gently turned me around. "I think here," I said as he hugged and kissed me again. I was in heaven.

Trey found the remote for his iPod and changed the music from Christmas carols to slow romantic ballads, the kind perfect for dancing. He reached for my hand. "Care to join me?"

He spun me around before gently grabbing onto my waist. At first, we danced at a normal space apart but as we became closer and closer, we could feel the beats of each other's heart. I breathed a deep sigh. I've never been bitten by the love bug so hard and so fast. I know I should be cautious about letting go of my heart, but that idea was already three sheets to the wind. I've fallen and fallen hard.

Trey stopped dancing and pulled me into him as tight as he could. He placed his lips at the base of my neck kissing me slowly until his lips touched mine. His kisses melted on my hot skin. I felt faint with desire. When our lips locked, neither of us wanted to let go. We were both swept away into another world by our passion.

A buzzer sounded and kept repeating until we finally heard it and let go of each other. We listened to it again as well as the loud chatter that filled the hallway. I stepped back, still shaken by my feelings and glanced at my watch. "Eight-thirty. That buzzer was the signal for all visitors to leave." I straightened my dress and ran my fingers through my now disheveled hair. "I guess I'd better go. As I said before, I don't want to wear out my welcome."

"You can never wear out your welcome with me. Call me so I know you got home safe. Please come back tomorrow. Jess, I love you."

I walked into the hallway and left for home with four other visitors, not wanting to call attention to my unkempt appearance.

CHAPTER 13

My life returned to normal chaos after last night's dreamy dinner date with Trey. Just thinking about him made me sigh. Our romantic dinner was like a scene from a movie. Since he liked the way I looked in a dress, I decided to wear something nicer than shorts and a T-shirt. I selected a pale pink lace short sleeve top and a short black skirt.

It seemed the more I learned about Trey the more I liked him, the more I respected his opinion, and the deeper I was falling in love with him. In so many ways, he was the polar opposite of Jake. Well-mannered, well-dressed and from what I could tell so far, not a liar. Not a liar; that's the most important point. I finished my morning coffee and a cinnamon bun before taking care of Sam. Since it was still early, and I finished Sam's morning routine, I thought I'd play around on my computer. Maybe I should try and write that novel. Well, maybe start with a short story first so I typed in a title, "Vacation Love."

Wow, this was sure a different way to start my day, but I knew I had plenty of time because I promised to visit Trey at four, not for dinner, but just for us to spend some time together. I worked hard on my story, but after writing only two hundred words, I looked at my desk clock. It was two thirty. I took Sam outside for his walk, changed and fixed my make-up ready to visit Trey. I knew if I walked Sam now, he could hang in there until we got home around six.

When we reached the rehab center, and after Sam received his hug from Skip, we walked into Trey's room. I was surprised to see him sitting on the edge of the recliner like he was ready to go outside wearing running shorts and shoes and a Cornell T-shirt. Checking his watch, he looked anxious to do something. He smiled at me, but his face lit up like a Christmas tree when Sam bolted over to him to get a hug.

"How's everything going?" I asked.

"Great," he responded. "I hope you like to walk. I know Sam does. Wait until you see how much stronger I am and how much faster I can walk even after only two days of therapy. My therapist attributes it to the fact that I worked out on a regular basis and was strong before the accident. He also suggested I might be able to leave rehab sooner than he and my doctor first thought because of that."

I smiled, trying to hide the fact I hated the thought of Sam and Trey going home at some point without me. We've become a threesome and I've loved every minute of it, but for now I had to push those sad thoughts aside and trust my heart and my feelings.

Trey stood and pulled out his walker. "I'm only taking this because the staff insists I do so for liability purposes. Just kidding, they want to keep me alive to so I can pay for their Christmas party tomorrow afternoon."

Nurse Sarah, who overheard him from the hall, popped her head in and laughed. "You got that right, Trey." She then walked into his room and announced, "Good news! Your doctor said you can go for a walk without the walker as long as you have someone with you. Both he and your physical therapist feel you are strong enough and have little or no risk of falling unless you're drunk or clumsy and trip over something." She laughed.

"That is good news," Trey responded. "Thank you." He was ready for this and didn't let the grass grow under our feet so as soon as Sarah left we made a quick exit out the building's side door. It was a beautiful Florida afternoon, warm with a light breeze. Sam lifted his nose in the air to feel the breeze as well as smell all the floral scents from the colorful plants surrounding the building. Trey glanced over at me and shot me a smile. He appeared happier than usual.

I held onto Sam's leash as tight as I could since we walked at Trey's brisk pace. "I'm impressed with your speed. You are getting stronger, but this isn't a race, just a nice casual walk for exercise," I reminded him.

He began to slow down and seemed winded. "Understood. I see Sam liked my pace."

I smiled. "When it comes to Sam, he loves everything about you and so do I." Sam heard his name and wagged his big furry tail.

Trey said, "By the way he looks at you, I can see he loves you too. Look guys, there's a lonely bench right over there waiting for us. Let's go pay it a visit. Shall we?"

We stopped our speed walking to head over to the bench. It was a perfect spot under a shade tree and off the walking path. Trey appeared a little less winded by now. "Are you sure you're all right?" I asked, concerned.

Trey answered still out of breath. "I'm good. I need time to exercise so I'll get better and stronger each day." Trey grabbed onto my arm as we sat down. He looked into my eyes.

"Jess, you look a bit pensive. Is everything all right? Can I help you with anything? I hope Sam's not becoming a problem for you." I smiled. "Neither you or Sam are a problem. You never could be." I leaned in and kissed his cheek. I hedged but knew I had to tell him about Jake. I couldn't keep it from him any longer. "You know, Trey, that Jake and I had been engaged for almost a year before I met you."

Trey looked puzzled. "I didn't know but hope you're not telling me this so you can go back to him."

"No. Never. He came to my house and asked me to give him back my engagement ring."

"He did? When did all this happen? You never told me about it." I felt I needed to explain further.

"I was wrong not to, but I so wanted to keep you healthy and stress free. I know you would have worried about me. He stopped by a few mornings back. My former diamond engagement ring belonged to his grandmother. Guess he wanted it back so he could propose to your nurse Barbie and give her the ring that has been in his family for years. I was surprised and didn't know what to do, but after giving it some thought, I gave it back to him. I don't wear it and no longer wanted it because both he and that ring now mean nothing to me."

Trey sat back still trying to catch his breath from our brisk walk. "Well, if this will make you feel any better, a wise woman once told me, 'You have to remove the old from your life to make room for the new.'"

I put my head on his shoulder. "That's a lovely thought and good advice and actually sounds pretty close to what my Granny Meta used to tell me. By chance, was this woman's name Granny Meta?" I laughed.

Trey remained curious. "No, but you must have inherited your smart genes from her to know that was the right response to help dump the past and move your life forward in a positive direction. And how did Jake respond? Did he leave like a gentleman or give you a hard time?"

"I remained firm and asked him to leave me alone. I needed you to know because, after all, Jake took care of you in the emergency room and Barb in the ICU. If it were not for their care, we wouldn't be together now. As for the diamond ring, I was relieved to remove it from my mind and heart. I need this chance for a fresh start in life and love."

Trey breathing easier replied, "A fresh start I hope for the both of us. You are as beautiful inside as you are out, but I already knew that. That's why I fell in love with you." Trey leaned in for a quick kiss. Sam lay at our feet enthralled by all the beautiful birds and the people walking by.

We sat and talked for about fifteen minutes. Trey appeared to be somewhat better so we talked about all kinds of things: politics, local charities, and Sam. Trey began to open up to me. "You know, Jess, I'm a certified workaholic. Because of that I never had time for dating. Not that I wasn't interested in finding that special person but usually my relationships lasted no longer than one dinner date. Since I've been spending so much time with you, I realize what I've missed, the companionship and friendship which at some point, as it did for us, turns into love. I'm so glad Sam brought us together. He did it in an odd way and through much hardship because of my accident, but sometimes the best things come out of the worst pain. You're the best thing that's ever happened to me in my entire life."

I was stunned into silence. After all he had just told me, I knew it wasn't his pain killers talking. I smiled and squeezed his hand. "Trey, I don't know what to say. I think you and Sam are very special and I love you both very much. You've brought so much happiness to my life especially when we're together."

I wiped a tear. "One month ago, my beloved dog Mazy died. I have missed her every day since. That's why Sam is like a breath of fresh air to my heart. I take care of him like he was my own dog. He's just so much fun. You are very lucky to have such a wonderful pet and the more I know about you, he's lucky to have you."

I paused. "But around the same time I lost Mazy, I had an

engagement broken off by a man I thought I wanted to spend the rest of my life with. He broke my heart into tiny pieces. The pain from that made me afraid to give my heart and love completely to anyone else. I didn't want to get hurt again. Funny, after last night's date and today hearing how much you love me, my heart opened up like the petals of a flower as a voice in my head told me to let go and fall in love with you."

Before I could say any more, Trey leaned in and placed a sweet kiss on my lips. Sam got excited watching us and whined a happy whine. When Trey's blue eyes looked directly into mine, my heart melted even more.

"Jess, I'm wearing my heart on my sleeve for you. I've never done this before for anyone else. I promise I would never hurt you. I treasure your love more than anything else in the world and want to be the man you choose to spend the rest of your life with. Please believe me. I have but a few days left in rehab before I move into my condo where we can spend more time together. I want to see you Christmas Eve and take you to Christmas dinner. I can't wait. Just the thought of that makes me heal faster."

I closed my eyes listening to his soft voice tell me how he felt about us. I opened them when he asked, "May I kiss you again?" I was eager to nod a "yes" after all one kiss from him is never enough and he did.

"I'm not going to let anyone as wonderful as you ever leave me. I've struck gold and want to keep you in my life after I leave here. Hey, smile, we'll be able to go on a proper date then."

That thought did make me smile. I liked the sounds of that. I winked, saying, "You do know how amazing last night's dinner was. I don't know how you can ever top that. It was the best dinner date I've ever had."

Trey wrapped his strong arms around me and gave me a big hug before we stood to walk back to his rehab building. He appeared better but still didn't seem right to me; he walked at a strong pace just a bit slower. When we reached his room, Nurse Sarah took one look at him and must have seen something wrong as well. Trey went to his chair and plopped down. Sarah came over and felt his forehead. "No fever, but we'll take it to be sure. You're looking a bit pale my friend." I decided to wait. Sam seemed fine with that. I gave him two cookies I had in my purse to hold him over until dinner.

"Your temp is spot on, ninety-eight point six." She held his wrist to check his pulse. "Your heart is racing like crazy. Maybe it's from too much exercise or too much daydreaming about Jess? To make sure you're okay, I'm going to get the blood pressure machine." Sarah left us for a few minutes.

Trey looked at me. "I'm fine. Please don't let this hold you two up."

I studied his reactions. "Do you feel lightheaded or dizzy? I'm concerned so we'll stay until Sarah comes back."

She returned and Trey knew the drill. He lifted his arm and placed it through the machine's cuff. "This will only take a few minutes. Try deep breathing," she advised him. Her eyes became large when she looked at the meter. "Your blood pressure is high. I'm going to call your doctor to see if I should administer any medication. Were you running?"

I interjected, "No, but he was walking briskly to try to increase his muscle strength. Do you think he overdid it?"

"That's possible," she answered. "He is on a few meds right now that could cause that kind of reaction to strenuous exercise. To be sure, I'd like to check with his specialist."

Sarah rushed off while Trey looked up at me and smiled. Sam pushed his way under Trey's arm. "Hey, you, don't worry. I'll be okay. I feel better already. I'm sure I just did too much. Workaholics are like that you know."

I hedged. "I don't feel right about leaving you in case you have something wrong."

Nurse Sarah came back into his room. "I called your doctor. He didn't want to add to your medications but advised me to monitor you for the next few hours and to make sure you have a light dinner."

Trey smiled. "See, Jess, I'll be fine. Now you can go home and get ready for Christmas Eve. I know you have a lot to do and besides I can't wait to come."

Sam gave his face a lick while I kissed the top of his head. "I'll call you in a little while. Please stay still for a while, maybe watch TV and try to relax."

He nodded. "I will."

Sam and I left for home relieved that Nurse Sarah was going to monitor him.

CHAPTER 14

With only two nights remaining after tonight to get ready for my open house, my thoughts swirled around in my mind like soft ice cream. The unfinished to-do list along with the butterflies in my stomach, made me wonder if I could complete everything on time. Rich and Terry volunteered to come over tonight and help move the furniture to make space for all of my company.

I knew it was too early for party set-up, but by working ahead, I'll have extra time to visit Trey in the rehab center. Traffic was dense on my way home from rehab probably due to all those holiday shoppers out for those last minute gifts. That reminded me I had no idea what to get Trey for Christmas. I took another sweet photo of Sam sporting a Cornell bandana I bought online. On one of my grocery runs, I had the store's photo shop print out an eight by ten enlargement on photo paper.

I bought a handsome frame made of different shades of wood perfect I thought for an office shelf or desktop. I didn't feel that was enough so I ordered some things online like a fancy pen and matching journal, and a key chain with Sam's photo. I plan to make a surprise gift bag for him. Good thing,

I already had Sam's big win from the pet store party all wrapped and ready to put under the tree. I don't know when I'd have time to shop now.

I looked at my watch. I was already an hour late to meet Terry and Rich. As we pulled into the driveway, the beauty and colors of those holiday lights transported me into a state of calm. I looked through my front windows and noticed Terry and Rich were already here and waiting. I'll have to explain what happened to Trey and why I'm so late. Sam and I walked around the yard so he could do his business first before going inside. I opened the front door to, "Well, it's about time you two showed up. What took you so long?"

I took a deep breath. "I was concerned about Trey. He became extremely winded and his blood pressure shot up after a short walk. I had to stay to see what was wrong. After checking with his doctor, the nurse said they would monitor him tonight."

Terry laughed. "Trey has to be fine. We want to meet this guy at the party. Now where and how would you like us to start?"

I sized up the layout of my living room with my eyes before asking. "Would you mind if I fed Sam first?"

Rich chuckled. "Not at all. How about feeding us as well?"

I was mortified. I didn't stop for anything. I lost my mind and forgot especially after Trey was not well.

Terry then confessed, "We called rehab when you were so late worried you were in an accident. The nurse on duty said you were still in Trey's room while his nurse took some tests. So we put two and two together and got six. Rich whipped up his famous chicken noodle casserole with homemade biscuits and a salad. We set your kitchen table so go feed our big guy first. The casserole is staying warm in the oven."

Tears in my eyes, I knew how lucky I was to have these guys in my life. I went into the kitchen. They all followed especially Sam. He was more than likely starving by now. I looked at my neighbors. "You two are so good to me. Thank you. Rich's chicken noodle casserole is one of my favs."

Sam ate like he had never seen food before. We did too. Everything was so yummy especially the biscuits. Our dinner break over, we went to work.

"I think we should make as much space as we can in my living room. Maybe we'll push the couch and chairs against the walls. They have wheels on their legs so it shouldn't be too hard. I can even help."

Terry saluted. "Aye. Aye. Captain."

I helped move the two chairs while they pushed the couch. Sam looked puzzled, probably wondering what was happening in Sam's world. I added.

"I have some metal folding chairs in the small shed behind the cottage. We can bring them in tomorrow and put them in the hall against the wall. Now, let's go do the same to the dining room."

Terry and Rich rubbed their hands together like they were ready to go. I continued. "I think all we have to do is take the four chairs away from the table and store them in my bedroom, which is a mess by the way, so don't look around too much. The dining table we'll use for the buffet like we did last year. I'll find my holiday tablecloth and will use that beautiful angel that came with Trey's basket for my centerpiece."

The guys looked pleased. "Well, you're easy. Really, except for the folding chairs and setting up the tablecloth, we can finish everything else tonight."

We worked about another half hour before Rich went back into the kitchen and called out.

"Almost forgot. Dessert anyone?"

Dessert? When on earth did he have time to do that? Terry and I proceeded into the kitchen to find a small sliced black and white loaf cake with chocolate frosting on my kitchen table next to paper plates and napkins. That cake was so moist and the frosting so fudgy, I exclaimed to Rich, "I'm in cake heaven." We devoured the entire loaf in record time.

Terry and Rich left soon after dessert. I thanked them and gave them each a big hug before they did. Sam and I took our evening stroll through all the lights before we returned home to get ready for bed. It was a long, nerve-wracking afternoon with Trey's changed condition.

Once back inside, Sam and I went into my bedroom. I called Trey from there to check on him. I must be exhausted since it's only nine forty-five and I'm in bed. Trey answered but his voice didn't sound as strong as usual. "How are you feeling," I asked.

"Well, I am less winded. I'm sure a good night's sleep will cure what ails me. But I am hungry. When the nurse said I'd have a light dinner that was an understatement. Now your turn, what have you been up to?"

"Terry, Rich, and I moved the living room and dining room furniture to make room for my Christmas Eve guests. Before that, Rich brought over dinner."

"Something good? I'll bet good enough to make me drool?"

"I won't say. But yes it will. Get a good night's sleep so you'll feel better tomorrow. I love you. Sam loves you." I blew a loud kiss through the phone.

"And I love you. I hope I'll see you tomorrow even if it's only for a short time."

"You will. You can't get rid of us that easily. Goodnight my handsome prince."

We hung up, leaving me with delicious dreams of seeing him tomorrow.

That night, realizing my party was less than two days away, I tossed and turned and had trouble falling asleep. I closed my eyes trying to think about my dream lover but as I fell into a deep sleep, my dreams shifted from one crazy thought to another. In my first dream, I welcomed my party guests with moisturizer slathered all over my face and wearing my black Halloween pajamas. What a nightmare! I shot up in bed telling myself my mind was worried about not being ready in time. I looked at Sam who was still snoring so I took a deep breath and went back to sleep.

At first, my next dream was peaceful. I envisioned Trey and I sitting on the same park bench as we did on our last walk. He had the same clothes on, running shorts and shoes, but I had on a fancy turquoise lace evening dress with matching heels. He smiled at me but had a blank stare when he looked into my eyes. I shook him and yelled at him to notice my dress. No matter how much I yelled, he couldn't hear me. He still had that same blank stare. Finally frustrated, I screamed at him as loud as I could. "Trey, wake up. Wake up!"

I must have screamed out loud because I woke up with Sam on top of me licking my face. My heart raced; my mind became frantic with worry. I hugged that big teddy bear of a dog, gave myself a few minutes to compose myself before getting dressed, ready to take Sam out for his walk. I'm sure it was just a nightmare probably from eating too much cake last night but no matter how hard I tried, I couldn't erase those thoughts from my brain.

Sam and I finished our morning walk and came back inside to have breakfast, even though I wasn't hungry. To take my mind off of that awful dream, I went to my computer to check for any work-related e-mails. Thank goodness there were none but I did receive a whole bunch of RSVPs for the party. Many included what dishes my guests would bring to share and, even though I had trouble finishing my cereal, the thought of all that delicious homemade food now made me hungry and my stomach rumble like a race car.

Sam wandered around the living room and dining room trying to get used to the new lay-out. I wondered how he would react to all the changes and if they might be upsetting to him especially after all he's been through, so I got up to walk over and pet him. Just as I stroked him, my cell buzzed.

I raced back to my desk and looked at the number "Barbie." Why would she be calling from her personal number? We're certainly not friends so I wondered if it was about Trey. "Hello, Barbie. Is everything all right?" There was dead silence on her end.

"Jess, I'm calling you about Trey." My heart felt heavy like a rock that dropped to the bottom of the deepest abyss in my body.

"Trey?" I blurted out. "What's wrong? Has something happened to him? When I left him last night, he seemed to be feeling better. Please tell me."

When Barbie didn't respond fast enough, my head throbbed like my blood vessels were ready to burst through my forehead.

Barbie continued. "Trey passed out this morning after breakfast. He was taken from rehab to the emergency room where Jake took care of him. He arrived unresponsive but Jake said he brought him around quickly. Evidently, Trey became lightheaded and fainted. Jake told me Trey needed to be observed further because of his recent head trauma so he sent him back up to ICU and Nurse Andrews. Jake advised me to call you STAT. He said when Trey opened his eyes after having fainted, all he could say was 'Jess.' He kept repeating your name. Jake said Trey's vitals were strong, but he still remains groggy."

My hands shook so much I could barely hold my cell up to my ear as she continued. "It's my day off, but I'm going to ICU to check on him now. Trey is Starra's and my patient. As his ICU nurse, I want to assist him in any way I can. Come as soon as you can. I'll be there when you arrive. Please be careful driving. You know we'll take the best care of him until you get there."

My mind couldn't process what Barbie just told me. My dream in which Trey wouldn't answer me may just have happened in real life. I now find the man I want to marry, and he passes out needing more tests to see why and if this could happen again because of his recent head trauma.

I wanted to cry or scream as loud as I could but pulled myself together to advise Barbie. "I'll be there as soon as I can. I just have to change and call Terry to watch Sam. I'll go straight up to ICU and ask for Nurse Andrews."

Barbie replied, "See you there. What happened to him may be a fluke incident. I'm sure his doctors will get to the bottom of this. Starra and I both care about his welfare."

After we hung up, my fingers were so weak I couldn't operate the keys on my cell. I needed to reach Terry but wanted to open my front door and to yell out to him "Help."

I dialed Terry's number. I heard his phone ring. "Please answer. Please answer. I need you," repeated in my mind. Oh no! His phone went straight to voice mail. I felt like throwing up. Then out of the blue, he picked up and interrupted his recorded message. "Jess? Are you all right?"

"Oh thank goodness you're home," I replied. "I received a call from Barbie this morning. Trey's in the ICU again. He fainted after breakfast and was taken to Healthwell's emergency room. She said he's conscious but groggy and his condition needs further observation. I have to go see him."

As Terry answered, I envisioned Terry wrapping himself in his superhero cape. "I'll be right over. Just get ready to go."

I cried sobbing into the phone. "Thank you…"

Terry repeated. "Jess, pull yourself together. We're all here for you. Now go get ready and leave ASAP. Sam will be okay alone for a few minutes. I'll let myself in. You gave me a key remember?"

I did remember. Who wouldn't give your superhero a key? I didn't want to take the time to change and couldn't care less what I looked like. If ever there was a time I wished I had wings and could fly, this was it. I arrived at Healthwell and raced into the building. The front desk was busy giving out visitor passes so I brushed by remembering I still had my old pass in my purse. I stuck it to my T-shirt hoping no one would notice the incorrect date and went straight to the elevator. I couldn't wait a second longer to see Trey. If anyone stopped me, I would play dumb saying that I thought hospital passes were good forever.

I went up to ICU. I saw Barbie in casual clothes standing with some nursing students showing off that diamond ring. I could hear the younger women giggling. "Boy, that Jake is one clever guy. You mean to tell me he slipped that ring along with a note to propose into a fortune cookie for you to open in a Chinese restaurant? He must be one knight in shining armor." Barbie nodded as I thought wait until that armor starts to rust. I was in no mood for their frivolities. Trey was in trouble and I needed to know how bad it was. I spotted Nurse Andrews behind the nurses' station. She didn't see me at first but after she did, she came rushing out to hug me. "Trey's vitals are still strong and he's awake. His doctors are examining him now to see why this happened. As soon as they leave, I will make sure you know how Trey's exam turned out before Barbie or I sneak you into his room. We hope by hearing your voice, he will become more alert and feel better. Now please sit in the waiting room and cover up that expired badge girl."

She waved her finger like I was a bad girl and made me laugh even if only briefly. My heart pounding, I saw his doctors come out of his room. They spoke to Nurse Andrews and wrote on his chart at the front desk before leaving. She walked over to tell me what his doctors said. They informed her that fainting or passing out was not an uncommon occurrence after his recent head trauma and especially if he had overexerted himself or stressed himself in any way. His medication may have elevated his blood pressure, and if he had not been eating properly, his blood sugar may have dropped too quickly. All could contribute to his condition, but they ordered lab tests to confirm the root of his problem.

Once gone, Barbie, now behind the nurses' station, signaled for me to come. I followed her into Trey's room. Hooked up to monitors and an IV, he looked like when I saw him on that first day. I walked over to his bed, leaned down, and whispered in his ear, "Trey, can you hear me? I'm here with you. I love you." I kissed his forehead. "Please let me know you're all right. This is a heck of a way to tell me you're not coming tomorrow night."

Nurse Andrews adjusted his IV to increase his fluids. I touched his forehead and he moved his head to look into my eyes. The two nurses looked at me as Barbie commented. "You may be just the medicine he needs."

I squeezed his hand and still a little groggy, he squeezed back and smiled. I told the nurses I would stay with him. Nurse Andrews said, "Please talk to him as much as you can. Tell him stories about Sam or maybe about your plans for Christmas. We have to leave to take care of other patients, but I will make sure the doctors know I approved your visit."

I sat with Trey for a few more minutes before I heard. "I'm still coming tomorrow night, you know. I wouldn't miss spending Christmas Eve with you for the world."

His eyes were wide open, and he held onto my hand. He looked into my eyes, taking them captive with his gorgeous blue ones and said, "Jess, don't leave me. I felt like you were here with me the entire time even in the emergency room."

I was so happy I kissed his lips and rang for a nurse. Both Barbie and Nurse Andrews raced into his room. They saw his eyes wide open, his demeanor alert, and that he was smiling at me. Starra asked, "Is everything all right? I called for his doctor the second you called. Trey, I see your eyes are open. Can you hear me? You gave us quite a scare. We didn't know if passing out was related to your head trauma."

Trey shot her a faint smile. "I can hear you as clear as a bell as well as my empty stomach rumbling."

We all laughed in relief. His doctor entered the room so I left. Standing by the doorway, he told Nurse Andrews that Trey's tests came back normal. He advised her. "We found no evidence of a blood clot or stroke. He more than likely overexerted, didn't eat his dinner, and as I said before, his blood sugar dropped causing the incident. I ordered breakfast for him. As long as he takes care of himself and pays attention to our instructions he should be fine."

I snuck as close to that doorway as I could and after overhearing their entire conversation, added. "I'll make sure he does."

His doctor laughed. "As my mother always said, a good man needs a good woman to keep him in line."

As soon as his doctor left, I returned to Trey's bedside. Tears of joy ran down my cheeks as I advised him. "Trey, you were lucky this time, but you really do have to follow the doctor's instructions and get better. This isn't a race. I love you and will be here for you for as long as it takes. You promised you would never leave me or Sam."

"And I didn't leave you. This morning, I felt weak and all of a sudden passed out. I still want to come to your Christmas Eve open house."

Nurse Andrews interrupted, "Your doctor thinks your fainting spell may be related to your overdoing it on your recent walk. You are in no condition to leave the hospital. You weren't really planning on going to Jess' party were you?"

Trey responded. "Yes, I was. Jess has an open house for anyone on the island who has no one to share the holiday with or no place to celebrate. I want to help her and spend Christmas Eve with both Jess and Sam."

Nurse Andrews paused and looked at me. "How about someone who lives off the island? My kids are grown and scattered, and I live alone. I don't even have a cat. May I come?"

I responded at once. "Yes. Please come. I'd love to welcome you to my home. My open house starts at five thirty. We start with appetizers and drinks before sharing a casual buffet dinner around eight. I'll write down my address for you. You already have my cell number."

Trey smiled. "That's my Jess. Can I come too?"

Barbie stopped him. "I don't think your doctor will approve your request. Jess' open house is only tomorrow night and may now be too early for you to leave the hospital."

An attendant entered with a food cart. Trey sat up on the side of his bed and opened the lid. "Now that's what I'm talking about, bacon and eggs and toast."

While he enjoyed breakfast, Nurse Andrews asked me, "What can I bring? I'd like to bring something."

I replied, "Starra, you've been so good to us. Just bring yourself and let me take care of you for a change. Who knows, this may become a yearly tradition for you?"

The good nurse smiled. "That's very nice but I'm sure I'll think of something extra special to bring. I'm excited and looking forward to it especially since I'm on duty Christmas Day. I like to cover for the young mothers so they can stay home with their kids."

"Starra, you are wonderful." I took out a small notebook from my purse and wrote down my address with directions from the hospital and handed it to her.

"If it's okay, I'll stay with Trey today for as long as I can. I'll just have to check in with Terry so he knows what's going on. I left him with Sam and most of the work for tomorrow night. If Trey's still here in the hospital tomorrow, I might have to ask Terry to host it with Rich."

I left the room to call Terry and fill him in. He said, "Don't worry about anything, Sam and I are fine. I'm having a blast fixing things for the party. Wait until you come home and see what I've done."

As soon as I entered Trey's room, he shook his head. "No, I will not let you miss your party. Jess, you have to be there. Even if I'm not strong enough to attend, you should hostess. It's your tradition."

"We'll see," I replied as I noticed he cleaned his breakfast plate like Sam does his bowl. That's a good sign. I stayed with Trey and we watched the movie "Elf" on TV. His coloring was so much better after he ate lunch. At four, Starra came into his room, advising, "Jess, I hate to ask you to leave, but Trey should really get some extra rest. Thank you for coming."

I understood and kissed him. "I'll call later. Please eat all your dinner and try to get some rest. Getting better is not a race. It's a slow journey or you can't win. Be good."

I waved and left for home, relieved Trey was all right.

CHAPTER 15

I woke up and checked my cell, relieved there were no messages from Barbie or Nurse Andrews. I took care of Sam before looking at what my amazing two superheroes had accomplished in my absence. Folding chairs were inside, holiday tablecloth found and put on my dining room table along with that gorgeous angel in the center. They placed the plastic cups, utensils, and paper plates on the far end of the table.

I looked at my front hall. My huge wicker basket, filled with eighty small wrapped gifts, took center stage on my front hall table. Rich left me a note that he was bringing over his long folding table to set up as a temporary bar. Some of my guests bring liquor and wine to share and I use up whatever I have on hand.

Terry popped his head in my kitchen door. I sighed. "I can't ever thank you both enough."

"No problem," he replied, laughing. "Just name your first born twins after us. Terry works for either gender. You are planning to see Trey today, *nes pas?*"

"Yes. I'm going in this morning. If he's in good shape, I'll come home by three."

Terry reassured me. "No hurry to come home. We'll be just fine."

I left for the hospital, dug out my expired pass, and went straight to his room. Nurse Andrews greeted me. "I want you to know I added you to his list of visitors since you're his only one and have his dog. He's waiting, excited to see you."

Trey surprised me. He was dressed, sitting up, and eating another hearty breakfast of bacon and eggs. He looked rested and healthy. His irresistible blue eyes looked into mine. "Hi sweetie, you look tired. I'm probably wearing you out considering all the tasks you have to finish for the party tonight. I must be getting better because they're taking me for a slow walk around this the floor later. I may not make it to the open house tonight but am working on taking you to Christmas dinner."

I smiled at his determination. "You know I can come here and see you tomorrow. I can bring any kind of take-out you want or maybe some great left-overs from the party?"

"I know," he added munching on a piece of bacon. "But a promise is a promise."

Nurse Andrews smiled, shaking her head. "Not so fast, my friend. That's what got you here. Besides, as long as you two are together for Christmas, it doesn't matter where that is."

Trey looked and sounded so much stronger, it's almost like his fainting incident never happened. I left him at two, not because of what I had to finish for the party, but because his doctor along with Nurse Andrews and Barbie chased me out. Barbie puzzled me. She told me after I arrived that she had today off but had to come in to assist a patient. Right before I left, Trey shot me a wink. "Look for a surprise delivery at six tonight, one for you and one for Sam from the Santa Express, but no peeking inside them until Christmas morning."

A surprise delivery? What did he do now? I knew I had to leave so I called back, "Trey, I'll call after the delivery arrives."

"I'm looking forward to it," he replied. I blew him a kiss saying, "Merry Christmas Eve. I'd love to stay here and spend it with you, but I already had this open house planned."

Nurse Andrews interrupted. "We know and I, for one, am looking forward to it. My shift ends at six so I should be at your house by seven. I know you said not to bring anything, but I'm sure I'll think of something special to bring by then."

She turned, drew the curtain around Trey's bed, and stepped inside with his doctor and Barbie.

Elated he improved, but sad and disappointed we'd be apart on Christmas Eve, I left for home.

By the time I got home, Terry and Rich had finished setting up everything. They even placed a white cloth toilet seat cover in the guest bathroom with a cartoon Santa covering one eye with "No Peeking" written across it. It's amazing I had enough time to freshen up and change, let alone glaze my large ham and place it in the oven, but I did. Thank goodness Rich and Terry stayed home with Sam because Rich accepted an unexpected delivery from The Island Grocery of two massive deli platters and rolls Jake had pre-ordered for the party. They were so large that Rich had to tilt them to fit them in my fridge.

As soon as we finished placing the rolls and condiments on the food table, happy party goers began to trickle in at five-thirty on the dot. Some brought hot appetizers, while others casseroles, all of which I kept warm in my oven. Good thing I cleaned out my fridge so I could store all the pasta, potato salads, and coleslaw.

Many bottles of wine and different kinds of liquor appeared on my bar table next to whatever liquor I had on hand. I set out the mixers, plastic cups, and ice. I looked up at my wall clock. It read six o'clock. I heard a knock on my front door. That was odd because everyone knew I left the door unlocked.

After hearing another knock, I opened the front door to find a delivery person in her online company's uniform placing two large cardboard boxes near my door. One was addressed to Jess Munroe and the other to Sam Musgrove. I signed for them and called Rich over to help me move them into my bedroom. We finished and my cell buzzed. I read a text message from Trey. "Did Santa deliver the packages yet? No peeking until tomorrow morning."

I texted him back. "They just arrived. Thank you. I can't imagine what's packed in those huge boxes, especially Sam Musgrove's. Cute. Love you."

He sent back. "Have fun opening them. I love you too. Bye."

By now it was six-thirty and more guests bearing food began to trickle in. We had already accumulated enough food to feed an army. Lucky for me, Rich and Terry were on kitchen duty and took care of everything. I knew I had to get back to my guests, many of whom came over to me to tell me how wonderful everything was. That made me so happy especially since I had to leave Trey. By now, it was almost seven and the front door opened. Jake arrived with Barbie who enjoyed showing off her engagement ring to anyone who'd give it a look. Because she helped Trey, I'm glad she only had to work the early shift so she could come.

Sam made his rounds to get petted. He was in doggie heaven because some guests brought treats for him. I had to take them and stash them up on my bookcase so he wouldn't try to tear all the boxes open. The party was great. Everyone was laughing and conversing in between bites of appetizers and drinks. All of a sudden, Rich stood in front of my Christmas tree and led the group in singing "Jingle Bells" with Sam assisting by shaking his collar. He announced that dinner would be served at eight.

Rich dashed home to pick up pans of his famous homemade lasagna. Everything was right on schedule. I glanced at my watch. It was seven. Seven? Where's Starra? I really wanted her to come. She didn't call to let me know otherwise so she must still be on her way. I'll give her another ten minutes to get here before I call her cell. Five minutes passed and I heard a knock on the front door. That must be her. I forgot to tell her I leave the door unlocked. Barbie walked over to stand next to me. I'm sure she wanted to welcome Starra as much as I did, but when I opened the door and saw who was staring at me, I gasped before putting both hands across my mouth surprised out of my mind. When I removed my hands, I yelled so loud I was sure everyone in the neighborhood could hear me. "They're here! He's here! It's Starra and Trey!"

Everyone quieted down and turned to take a look. Still in shock, I remained frozen staring at Trey standing on my front door mat with a walker and Nurse Andrews holding onto his arm. She was not in uniform and looked pretty in a red and green plaid party dress. Realizing this wasn't a dream, I hugged Trey as I asked Starra, "How is this even possible?"

Starra winked. "I told you I'd think of something special to bring. I hope this is special enough."

I held back tears of joy. "It sure is. This is by far the most wonderful Christmas surprise I've ever had." Sam spotted Trey and raced across the room to greet him. He sniffed the walker and did not jump up on him.

Trey laughed. "For me too. This idea was all Starra's. She needed Barbie's help to pull this off. That's why Barbie came in on her day off today. May we come in or should we celebrate out here on your front porch?"

"Oh yes, come in. Please come in and meet everyone."

Trey added, "We both should thank Nurse Andrews and Barbie who asked for special permission from my doctor. He told them that as long as I took it easy and didn't drink any alcohol, I could stay until ten. Besides I have my own private nurses along side of me. I found out I was coming after Starra came into my room tonight all dressed up and asked me for a favor. She said since she had no one to escort her to your open house would I be so kind to do so. I thought I was dreaming and couldn't believe she had just asked me that. Needless to say, I dressed as quickly as I could."

I covered my mouth with my hands to quell any more screams of joy. Once calmer, I told Starra, "You and Barbie are my guardian angels. This is the best 'something special' ever! Now please let me introduce you and Trey to everyone."

Sam and I followed Starra and Trey around the small rooms trying to introduce them to as many guests as I could. Terry and Rich rushed over to meet Trey. "Nice to finally meet the guy who stole our Jess' heart. We have some great appetizers and drinks. Dinner will be served soon."

Starra helped Trey over to a chair as many of my guests walked over to greet them. I kissed the top of Trey's head before I left them to their new friends. "I have to help set up dinner. Stay put. I'll be right back."

Starra asked, "Anything I can do to help?"

I smiled. "You've helped me more than you could imagine." Trey looked around at my house. "I love your home. You do make Christmas special. I brought a special after dinner treat for you."

I was happy just to have him here, he was my special treat. We all ate a wonderful holiday buffet. I made up a plate for Trey and took mine to sit with him. "Jess, this beats the heck out of hospital food."

Starra, sitting next to Jake and Barbie, enjoyed her dinner as well. She came over to tell me. "Thank you for inviting me, Jess. You know I would have been sitting home alone. I'm so happy, I feel like I'm celebrating Christmas right now with you and Trey."

Rich and Terry walked by and winked at Starra. "Don't forget you're celebrating with us too." Rich laughed.

The food was delicious. The lasagna, the deli sandwiches, the salads, my ham, and those fresh baked rolls. I could go on about all the amazing dishes my fellow islanders brought to share. We all ate until we had passed full.

As I stood to put away any leftovers, Terry touched my shoulder. "We've got this. Trey's here for a short while longer. You should stay here with him. I saw you bought aluminum foil pans to put the extra food in. Don't worry, we'll do that and set up dessert when we're done."

Trey overheard Terry. "Rich and Terry are great. Since you don't have to serve dessert, I have a special dessert for you. I'd like to get down on one knee to give it to you, but since I may not be strong enough to get back up on my own and I don't want to hurt Starra, I'll give you my surprise right here."

Everyone in the room must have heard him because they all became very quiet. Trey reached in his pocket and pulled out a small velvet emerald green box. Reaching for my left hand, he asked, "Jess, I realize we've only known each other a short time, but I know I love you more than life itself and want to spend the rest of my life with you. Will you marry me?"

I gasped. It seemed like everyone else in the room did too at the same time, waiting for my answer. "Yes," I gushed. "Yes. I will."

Sam, who lay by our feet, jumped up and licked the both of us because we were so happy. Trey opened the ring box and I viewed a gold ring with a very large square cut emerald at its center surrounded by smaller sparkling diamonds. As he placed it on my ring finger, he said, "Remember I told you to get rid of the old in your life, so you could welcome new? The new is my great grandmother's emerald and diamond ring. I hope you like it."

"Like it. I love it!" I exclaimed.

We then were mobbed with happy well-wishers wanting to meet Trey and see my ring. Even Jake and Barbie congratulated us. For some unknown reason, Terry grabbed a bag of soft fake snowflakes leftover from party decorating and sprinkled it over us while holding a branch of mistletoe with his other hand. He led the entire group in "Auld Lang Syne." I looked at my ring and told Trey, "It's so beautiful."

He looked into my eyes and said, "And so are you."

Rich had to whistle for everyone's attention. "Our desserts are fabulous and on the dining room table. Please help yourselves and let's give our two love birds some privacy."

Everyone, including Starra, left the room to enjoy dessert. Trey and I remained alone together and kissed, knowing we didn't need mistletoe to celebrate only our love for each other.

THE END

Don't miss out on your next favorite book!
Join the Satin Romance mailing list
www.satinromance.com/mail.html

THANK YOU FOR READING

❄

Did you enjoy this book?

We invite you to leave a review at your favorite book site, such as Goodreads, Amazon, Barnes & Noble, etc.

DID YOU KNOW THAT LEAVING A REVIEW...

- Helps other readers find books they may enjoy.
- Gives you a chance to let your voice be heard.
- Gives authors recognition for their hard work.
- Doesn't have to be long. A sentence or two about why you liked the book will do.

ABOUT THE AUTHOR

Mariah Lynne takes readers on breathtaking adventures. Whether traveling through time, solving a crime, or finding love, her heroines are strong willed independent women whose memorable stories keep the pages turning.

A graduate of Syracuse University, Mariah resides on a beautiful Florida Gulf Coast island. Because she loves where she lives, Southwest Florida becomes the backdrop for all of her stories. Before writing fiction, she wrote weekly columns for two newspapers.

Mariah is a member of Romance Writers of America and Southwest Florida Romance Writers. An animal lover, she served three years on the board of directors for a county wide no-kill animal shelter.

Her books include PAWS for CHRISTMAS, THE DUCHESS' NECKLACE, SHADOWS ACROSS TIME, and THE LOVE GYPSY also available as an audio book. Her short stories "Love at First Flight" and "The Kaine Mutiny" are published in Vols. 1 and 2 of FROM FLORIDA WITH LOVE. "Claws for Justice" is included in NINE DEADLY LIVES a mystery anthology featuring cats.

When not writing, Mariah, a former video retailer, enjoys watching movies, traveling, swimming, and spending time with her husband. She still misses her amazing dolphin hunting dog Max, a shelter adoptee.

www.MariahLynne.com
MariahLynneAuthor@yahoo.com

facebook.com/MariahLynneAuthor

twitter.com/mariahlynne1

ALSO BY MARIAH LYNNE

Shadows Across Time

The Duchess' Necklace

Featured in the anthologies:

From Florida With Love: Sunsets & Happy Endings

From Florida With Love: Sunrise & Stormy Skies